NORTHBOUND

INTO THE WILDERNESS

by

Judith Huntley

Published By

Eighth Street

Washington

Edited by Alisa Carter
Designed by Linda Jo Huber
Maps by Linda Jo Huber

*Back cover photo: from U.S.G.S. Department
of the Interior, Peter Haeussle, photographer.*

Eighth Street
Washington

Manufactured in the United States of America

ISBN-13: 978-1480144842

ISBN-10: 1480144843

DEDICATION

To John Huntley for always encouraging me to dream big and to have the courage to make those dreams come true and to my wonderful children, Bob and Mark who have been loving and supportive throughout this amazing journey.

ACKNOWLEDGMENTS

My thanks to all my family and friends who supported me through the process of completing this book.

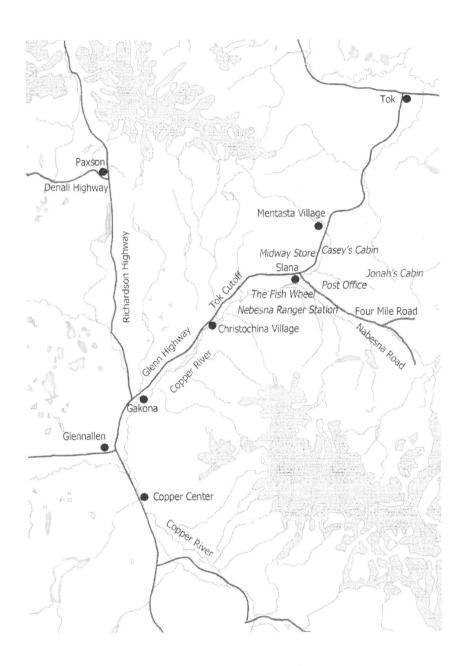

Copper River Valley - Interior of Alaska

Contents

Chapter One: Casey's Dream

After five hours of traveling over the open road, listening to the dull roar of the engine in her eighteen-wheeler, Casey looked up into the dark northern sky. She tossed a few sunflower seeds into her mouth, yawned, and rubbed her tired eyes. What was that faint green glow in the distance that seemed to dance across the midnight sky, lighting up the entire summit? It grew brighter and then dimmed as it turned to soft shades of pink and yellow and then back to green. It shot straight up and then spread out, reaching for miles into the heavens. What could it be? She watched the glow as she approached the foothills leading up the side of the mountain. Grinding down from tenth to ninth and then eighth gear she began her descent. Her rig weighed 80,000 pounds, and it was going to take her forever to get to the peak where she could see the swirling lights better. She only hoped that the colorful glow would still be there when she reached the summit. She geared down to fifth, then fourth and eventually to third gear as she lugged her heavy load up the mountain.

After thirty minutes of dragging her heavy load, she made it to the summit, where another truck was already parked in the pullout. The driver was outside, standing on the grass and watching the light show. Casey approached him and asked, "Have you ever seen anything like these lights before?"

He answered, "Well, yes, I have, when I ran the Alcan Highway from Bellingham, through Canada and into Alaska. They're the Northern Lights or the aurora borealis; you can see them during the cold winter months. Usually they're not this bright until you drive further north. We're getting quite a show tonight."

They watched for another thirty minutes, and then the other driver left to drive down the mountain toward Tacoma to a nearby truck stop. Casey decided to park her truck in the pullout for the night so she could watch the swirling lights for a little while longer. She began to remember back several years ago when she was a girl of only fifteen and wanted to live in the wilderness of the last frontier in Alaska. She could have watched the northern lights all winter long right outside her cabin door if she could have lived there.

Enough dreaming, she told herself as she climbed into her truck to bunk down for the night. She fell asleep while dreaming of Alaska.

It was 5 a.m. when Casey woke to the powerful shaking of her truck and the sound of glass shattering; it was Mitch breaking into her truck with a crowbar. She was alone and terrified. There was no one else in sight.

Mitch grabbed her by her hair. "You will never get away from me. I will always find you. You belong to me." He shoved Casey against the bunk, looming over her as she crumbled to the floor. He continued to scream profanities at her as she lay at his feet, praying for him to leave. After what seemed forever, she heard no sound only her whimpering voice as she lay on the floor, afraid to move. Once she felt he was really gone, she pulled herself up and looked outside to make certain he wasn't lingering. After a few anxious moments, she let out a shaky breath and began searching around her truck for a broom and dust pan to clean up the broken glass. She looked out what used to be her truck window, searching the heavens for the northern lights, but they were gone. A feeling of despair swept over her and she began to sob.

When Casey met Mitch only two years ago, they both worked for the same trucking company as regional drivers, often swapping out loads or making deliveries at the same consignee. Even though they were solo drivers, they often ran together, keeping each other company, talking over their CB radios just to pass the time. Mitch seemed nice enough at first and always had respect for her as a solo truck driver—not always the norm for women driving over the road. It wasn't long before Mitch became obsessive and controlling, becoming angry if she even talked to another driver.

After pulling herself up off the floor of her truck, she washed her face and combed the glass out of her long brown hair. At forty years old, she had no intention of living in fear for the rest of her life. She was tired of wondering where he was or where he was going to show up next. Even when he wasn't harassing her, Casey felt like she had an extra pair of eyes watching her and lurking in the shadows of the night. She would find a way of getting away from him.

2

After starting the engine in her eighteen wheeler, she put her truck into first gear and released the air brakes. She pulled out onto the road and headed down the mountain to the closest truck stop to have her window repaired.

Casey was cautious as she pulled into the truck stop, checking out the fuel island and scanning the parking area for any sign of Mitch's truck. She backed into one of the parking spots to drop her load and bobtailed over to the repair shop. They could have her window replaced within a couple of hours— just enough time to get some breakfast and a hot shower. She put fresh clothes into her shower bag, climbed down the steps of her truck, and Mitch grabbed her from behind.

She let out a scream as she felt his cold, sweaty hand press down over her mouth. He dragged her by her hair between two parked trailers and slammed her body up against one of them. Pulling out a switch-blade knife, he gently rubbed it along the side of her face, giving her a gentle poke every few inches with the sharp point of the blade. She held her breath as tears ran down her face.

He whispered in her ear, "Is this the way you want it? I think you need to believe me when I tell you that you can't get away from me." He pinned her body up against the trailer door as he yanked her long hair back, exposing her neck. Laughing softly, he ran the knife blade down her neck until it reached the buttons on her shirt. He laughed as he popped off one button at a time until she was completely exposed. Slamming her down on the concrete, he yanked off her shirt and gave her stomach a swift kick. "I'll always be just around the corner waiting for you."

Casey sobbed, listening to his footsteps fade as he slipped away between the trailers in the lot. He was finally gone.

Terrified and humiliated, Casey pulled herself up, grabbing for her shower bag to find another shirt to cover herself with. She looked around and saw no one; she needed to get to the driver's lounge as fast as she could. She continued to weep as she shuffled through the parked trailers in the parking lot. As she passed through the door into the driver's lounge, she noticed blood dripping down her legs. Luckily she was able to get a shower room without having to wait. Shutting and locking the door behind her, she sat on the toilet seat sobbing for at least thirty minutes. At least she felt safe, even if it was only for a short time. It was another hour before Casey was able to clean herself up and another thirty minutes before she felt safe enough to leave the shower room.

She knew she needed to call dispatch to let them know that she would not be able to make her ETA on time. As she passed the driver's lounge, she glanced over at one of the tables and stopped dead in her tracks. A magazine with a picture of the northern lights on the cover lay on the table.

After talking to dispatch, she went by the table and picked up the magazine. Something about the picture seemed to pull at her. She decided to look it over as she had a hot meal in the truck-stop restaurant.

As she waited for her meal, she skimmed through the magazine until she came across an article about homesteading in the Copper River Valley of the Alaska wilderness, just like she'd dreamed of living off the land in the Alaska wilderness as a young girl. Remembering the beautiful aurora borealis dancing against the midnight sky when she was in her truck on top of the summit, she felt a glimmer of hope, and a little chill. First the picture of the northern lights, and now an article about looking for a change of lifestyle in the back woods of the Alaska frontier? It was like a sign. Could she really do it? Could she leave everything behind and disappear into the Alaskan wilderness?

She thought about Mitch, waiting in every truck stop, preying on her mind.

After doing a little research on the computer in the driver's lounge, she was ready to seriously consider it.

****

The next day, she decided to contact a realtor in the small rural town of Copper Center, Alaska. The following day, Mike Waller, a local realtor from the town of Glennallen, contacted her with a couple of pieces of property that she might be interested in. The one that was most appealing to Casey was a partially built cabin that sat on an acre of land facing the Slana River right next to the Wrangell-St. Elias National Park. The land and cabin were located in a small rural settlement called Slana right off the Tok Cutoff, about an hour and a half north of Glennallen.

Casey had a good feeling about the little cabin on the banks of the Slana River and was anxious to see it. It fit right in with her lifelong dream of living in a wilderness area in the Alaska frontier. The owner was asking $40,000, which fit into Casey's budget. Mike agreed to call Casey back tomorrow after he gained more information about the property from the owner.

Casey went back to driving her regular route while she waited for the realtor to call her back, watching around every corner for Mitch. Late that night she heard Mitch talking on his CB to another driver. Fear swept over Casey as she listened, trying to figure out his location. She was a good hour from the next truck stop. She had to keep moving and not say a word over the CB, letting him know of her location. Tears began to run down Casey's face as she saw a familiar truck coming up behind her. Her whole body began to shake as Mitch drove closer, coming within inches of the rear of her trailer. Casey felt sick to her stomach as she remembered Mitch abusing her in the truck parking lot only a few hours ago. She wasn't going to let that happen again. Suddenly, Mitch pulled out from behind and drove up on her left with less than a foot between their trucks. It was late at night and not many trucks were on the road, so he rode alongside of her, refusing to slow down or pass her by. When she slowed down or tried to speed up he kept his speed at the same pace. She tried not to let his intimidation get to her, but she was losing that battle quickly as he rolled down his window and drove his big rig even closer, laughing. Casey fought back the tears as she kept driving, trying to keep control of her own eighteen-wheeler. She slowed down, and finally another big rig came up behind her and Mitch had to move on. She stuck close to the oncoming truck until she finally made it to the truck stop, where she would not be alone. Mitch drove by her exit, but she knew not to trust that he wouldn't circle around and meet her in the parking lot again for another bout of his abuse. When she pulled into the fuel island, she asked the security guard to keep an eye on her truck during the night, and then parked in a well-lit area.

In the morning Casey's cell phone rang. It was Mike, ready to give her more information about the cabin and property. After spending an hour on the telephone with Mike, Casey learned that the acre of land was flat and partially cleared. The cabin faced the Wrangell Mountain Range, which stretched out as far as the eye could see. There were three impressive mountain peaks that could be seen across the valley on a clear day, Mt. Drum (elevation 12,010 feet), Mt. Wrangell (14,630 feet), the largest active volcano in the United States, and Mt. Sanford (16,237 feet). The mountains overlooked the beautiful

Copper River Valley, where the little cabin sat. Casey was excited and wanted to hear more. The location was exactly what she was looking for, but what condition was the cabin in? How much work needed to be done to make it habitable? The cabin was six hundred square feet with a large root cellar that would hold all the food Casey needed to store during the winter months. With Slana being in the interior of Alaska, winters would be bitter cold. When she asked Mike about the length of the cold winter months, he replied with a statement that Alaskans often use: "There are two seasons in Alaska—winter and getting ready for winter." Mike told her that temperatures were known to drop to negative seventy degrees during the brutal winter months. That wasn't about to stop Casey. She was not a stranger to hard work, and living over the road in her big rig wasn't always easy either, especially with Mitch stalking her. One of the deciding facts that sold Casey on wanting to see the property was that it was located on the Tok Cutoff, a paved road that the state would maintain and snow plow through the winter months. She was definitely interested in flying up to see this little piece of wilderness that could end up being hers. Within the next forty-eight hours, she was on an airplane flying toward Anchorage.

Casey standing beside her truck

Chapter Two: Trip to Glennallen

Two weeks later Casey was flying through the clouds on her way to Alaska, anticipating her arrival in Anchorage. She began realizing what a relief it was to leave dispatch and Mitch behind. For the first time in several weeks, she could relax. She took a deep breath, closed her eyes, and tried to visualize what life in the Copper River Valley would be like.

As Casey let her mind wander off, she could hear Mike Waller's voice: "People who chose to live in Alaska are either running away from something, or they are running toward something." She was definitely running away from something, but she was also running toward a dream she had had for as long as she could remember. She had always sought a simpler lifestyle that she couldn't find in a large metropolitan city. She had always dreamed of living off the land, being self-sustaining. Living in a remote wilderness area would allow her to feel connected to the wildlife as well as the vast Alaska frontier. Casey wasn't afraid of hard work, but she knew there would be challenges ahead of her. The hours went by fast as she gazed out the window into the clouds, wondering what kind of life was ahead of her.

Suddenly the pilot's voice spoke over the intercom. "If you look out the window to your right, you can see our airport moose grazing off to the side of the runway. He often greets our passengers to the wonderful state of Alaska."

Casey was startled awake. She looked down at her watch; three hours had passed and the aircraft was landing on the runway. The passengers were laughing at the pilot's moose comment when one of the Alaska residents shouted out, "There are lots of resident moose living around town. They feel safe from wild predators that live nearby. Be careful when driving—they like to cross the highway when you least expect them to."

The plane was on the runway and coming to a stop when Casey spoke to the woman next to her, who was also a resident of Anchorage. "I intend to take that warning seriously. I'm new to Alaska and will be traveling to Glennallen on

Highway One for the next few hours." Casey grabbed her carry-on bag from the overhead storage bin and reached into the side pocket for the state road map.

The woman smiled. "That's a five-hour drive from Anchorage to Glennallen. Are you going to stop for the night along the way?"

"Probably so; I need to pick up my rental car and get a bite to eat before I head out of town."

Casey and the woman exited the plane and walked toward the car rental stand. "There's a wonderful rustic lodge along the Glenn Highway, which is also known as Highway One," the woman said. "Sheep Mountain Lodge is nestled at the foot of Sheep Mountain, where you can see plenty of Dall sheep grazing on the nearby mountain ledges. It's about a three-hour drive from Anchorage. You could make it that far and drive into Glennallen tomorrow. They have a good restaurant with the best sourdough pancakes you ever tasted." She gave Casey the phone number of the lodge and told her to call for a reservation, because they book up fast during tourist season.

Casey took the number and thanked the woman as they said good bye. Within forty-five minutes Casey was in her rental car and headed out of town. She drove through Eagle River and stopped to fuel her rental car and have a fast-food hamburger at the local gas station. She took a few minutes to call Sheep Mountain Lodge to see if they had any vacancies for that evening.

"You're in luck," the clerk said over the phone. "We have one cabin open still. Would you like me to hold it for you?"

Casey sighed with relief. "Yes, please. I'm from the lower forty-eight and this is my first visit to Alaska. It will probably take me about three hours to get there, from what I've been told."

"I'll keep the candle burning in the window. The road along the Glenn Highway is windy and there are a few mountain passes you need to get through, but we have twenty-four hours of daylight this time of year, so it'll be a pleasant drive. Enjoy the scenery and I'll see you when you get here." He gave a chuckle and said, "Slow down, you're on Alaska time now."

Casey smiled. Everybody she'd seen in Alaska so far did seem to move at a much more relaxed pace. She was looking forward to that.

The weather was clear with no rain in sight, and Casey was grateful for Alaska's twenty-four hours of sunlight during the short summer months. The conditions were perfect for a beautiful drive through the mountains. Casey was a little tired from her flight, but she was up to the drive. After all, she was a truck driver, used to brutal hours of driving over the road. If she didn't make too many scenery stops along the way, she could make it to the lodge by 10 p.m. She was hoping for a couple of leisurely hours in the morning to spend over a hot breakfast and coffee. If she were lucky, she could get some pictures of the Dall sheep. Her appointment with the realtor was for 1 p.m, so time would not be an issue.

Casey began to relax and enjoy the beautiful scenery of one mountain after the next. The mountain peaks were still covered with ice and snow, and she could see where the gray rock led down to the tree line, where spruce and alders grew in abundance. She was leaving the larger towns behind her as she continued to drive into the interior of Alaska along the scenic mountain roads. She began to climb in elevation as she drove through the towns of Sutton and Chickaloon. As the road curved along the Matanuska River, she passed a couple of small settlements that weren't on the map, and she wondered if the small settlement of Slana would be similar.

Previously, Casey had done some research and knew that the Matanuska River separated the Talkeetna Mountains to the north and the Chugach Mountains to the south. As Casey began to drop in elevation, the magnificent Matanuska Glacier appeared. Her mouth dropped open. She had never seen a glacier before. She noticed a sign along the road that read "Glacier Park Resort," so she turned into the entrance for a closer look. She spotted a platform that allowed excellent views of the spectacular glacier, and a couple of short trails that would bring her even closer to the glacier, where she could take some great pictures.

As she began down the trail for a closer view, she thought she probably shouldn't take the time to hike down the path for a closer look, but she knew she might not get the opportunity to stop on her way back. As she came closer to the glacier, she could see that the color of the ice was a deep shade of sapphire blue. The glacier appeared to pour into a basin of gray silt, and beyond the silt was an extensive forest of short spruce, aspen, and birch with colorful wildflowers sprinkled throughout the foliage. Casey wanted to stay there forever, but she knew her time was limited and she needed to get back up the trail, but not without taking some stunning pictures of the glacier.

Within a couple of minutes she was back in her rental car and driving down the Glenn Highway, enjoying the scenic views as she drove along the curvy mountain road. Casey was an hour from Sheep Mountain Lodge and was looking forward to a good night's sleep. The road became even more windy and narrow with very steep mountain passes, but visibility was good because of the nice weather and constant sunlight. As she continued to drive up one of the mountain passes, she came to a place called Caribou Creek and began her decent down the steep mountain pass. In the distance she could see a lodge and a group of small, rustic cabins. As she approached the area, she saw a sign that read Sheep Mountain Lodge. Casey pulled in. In the main building she was greeted by the motel clerk, a man in his mid-sixties, dressed in faded overalls and a worn red and black flannel shirt that had seen better days. He was a true Alaskan Sourdough with salt and pepper hair that had grown down past his shoulders and matched the color of his thick, bushy beard.

As Casey walked up to the desk counter, the burly man asked, "Are you the woman from the lower forty-eight that I'm holding the cabin for?"

"Yes, that's me."

The old sourdough yawned. "Straight out that door and to the left; cabin number four. Here's the key. Breakfast at 6 a.m., sharp."

Casey followed with a yawn of her own. "I'll be here and with an appetite."

Even though it wasn't dark outside, the minute her head hit the pillow, she was asleep. Morning came abruptly when the alarm went off at 5:15 a.m. Casey was up and in the shower in five minutes. She was looking forward to the hearty breakfast the old man had promised her. It would be nice to relax for a couple of hours with a hot breakfast and coffee. As she walked over to the restaurant, she looked up on the face of the steep mountains to see if she could see any white specks that could possibly be Dall sheep. It was a little foggy, but the sun was already beginning to burn the morning haze off. Hopefully, after breakfast the sky would clear and she could see the sheep that roamed the steep mountain ridges.

Matanuska Glacier taken from the Glenn Highway

Matanuska Glacier

Casey smelled bacon and eggs as she entered the café and found a table by the window where she could have a clear view of the mountain ledges. She had already ordered coffee and sourdough pancakes when she noticed reindeer sausage on the menu. She decided to live dangerously and order a side of the sausage. After the waitress brought her breakfast, Casey was surprised to find that the sausage didn't have a gamey taste.

After an hour and a fourth cup of coffee, Casey decided to pay her bill and go looking for the Dall sheep. She asked the waitress if there was a nearby trail where she could get a better view of the mountain ridges. The waitress pointed out through the window to a short path leading up the side of the mountain that was only a mile long.

Sheep Mountain was an awesome sight with the Glenn Highway cutting right into the side of the mountain. The trail was narrow and steep, but it appeared to be a good path that would take her up behind the lodge. When Casey hiked up the trail and looked down over the lodge, she could view the whole side of the mountain and was able to view Caribou Creek in all its glory. There were birch and alder trees growing down by the river bed, but for the most part it was a rough, rocky terrain, the perfect home for the Dall sheep. Casey continued to climb the steep trail until she came upon a small clearing where she could stop and look around. There wasn't a lot of snow on the mountain tops, so the sheep would be up high, grazing where they felt more protected. During the winter when the mountains were covered with snow, the Dall sheep came down closer to the road where they could find vegetation to eat. About three quarters of the way up the mountain, small white figures moved along the path across the mountain ridges. Casey focused her camera on the white spots and used her high-power lens to get some great shots.

Her time was running short and she needed to get back on the road to make her appointment in Glennallen on time. By 10 a.m. she was back at the lodge, all packed up and checking out. It was hard to leave Sheep Mountain, but her time was limited—she had to return to the lower forty-eight in five days. Casey wondered if the Copper River Valley would be as beautiful as Caribou Creek. She arrived in Glennallen with fifteen minutes to spare.

Chapter Three: Introduction to Slana

Glennallen was located at the crossroads of the Richardson and Glenn Highways. It was the largest town (population two hundred and fifty) nestled in the heart of the Copper River Valley. Casey spotted the Visitor Center and made a mental note to herself to be sure and stop in after her meeting with Mike. It would be a good place to gather information about the surrounding area.

Mike was a tall, thin man in his early forties with sandy brown hair, a clean cut man, dressed in a pair of gray slacks and a plaid shirt. When Casey walked through the door, she noticed a moose head and the head of a Dall sheep mounted on the wall. On the opposite side of the wall was a full-size grizzly bear skin.

Casey was taken aback. She couldn't understand why anyone would want to kill such awesome animals and display them in such a manner.

When Mike saw Casey staring at his trophy's with an appalled look, he said, "My family and I live a subsistence lifestyle, as do so many Alaskans who chose to live in the bush. I don't kill for the trophy; I kill for the meat to feed my family."

Casey realized there would be many things to learn living out in such a remote area. A city lifestyle was so different than a lifestyle found in rural Alaska where people were living off the land.

Mike smiled. "You must be Casey, the truck driver from outside who is interested in the Slana property. It's a nice piece of property; an acre of land with a partially built cabin, right on the Slana River. You'll never go hungry if you like fish. The Slana River has a lot of burbit and kings."

"I love to fish almost as much as I love to eat them. I've always wanted to live off the land in a remote wilderness area of Alaska. I've come a long way to make that dream come true."

Mr. Waller suggested that they take a drive to Slana and meet Linda Jo, the owner of the property. He had previously set up an appointment with her for that afternoon, knowing that Casey needed to return to the lower forty-eight as soon as possible. Slana was an hour and a half northeast of Glennallen, located on the Tok Cutoff. Mike suggested they pick up a couple of sandwiches at The Hub, the local gas station in town, and then they could be on their way.

Mike filled his gas tank, bought a couple of sandwiches, and they headed north on the Richardson Highway. They drove about twenty minutes when they came to Gakona Junction, where there was a small store with a few groceries, a telephone, and the last place to buy gasoline for a very long time. They turned northeast on the Tok Cutoff and drove forty-five minutes when they came to an Athabascan settlement called Chistochina.

"Chistochina is an Ahtna village that has been in the Copper River Valley for many generations," Mike said. "The village is run by the elders of the tribe, and they have their own tribal police and small school house where grades K through eight are taught. Athabascan natives also live in Slana and can be found up and down the Tok Cutoff. The Ahtna people are proud people. They follow many of the old ways and traditions and enjoy a subsistence lifestyle."

Casey listened intently to the history Mike was sharing with her. Life in rural Alaska was so different than anything she could have imagined. She felt like she was traveling back in time as they continued the drive to Slana. Right about that time Mike dropped his little bomb, informing Casey there was no electricity along the Tok Cutoff. She knew Slana was in a remote area, but no electricity? How do people live without electricity? Mike explained that most people have generators that run off diesel fuel and make electricity. That was interesting to Casey. She was going to have a lot to learn if she decided to make Slana her home.

Ten minutes later Mike made a right turn onto Nebesna Road. As they passed a rustic log cabin, Mike said, "That's the Nebesna Ranger Station. You can get a lot of good information about the Slana area from the ranger. If you look straight ahead, you'll be looking at the edge of the Wrangell-St. Elias National Park, one of the wildest parks in America. The National Park and Preserve is the home of more glaciers than any other park, with mountain peaks reaching over 16,000 feet. Mount St. Elias is over 18,000 feet, the second tallest after Denali. It is an impressive sight." Mike smiled. "The property you're thinking about purchasing borders this park."

She could only imagine looking out her cabin window, staring past the Slana River, pine trees whistling in the gentle breeze coming off the river. These majestic mountains , in all their glory, would be in her backyard.

Next they made a left turn into a gravel parking lot and saw a small log building with a sign that read U.S. Post Office. Linda Jo, a tall husky woman, was at the door waving, calling out, "I'm just closing up for the day. Give me a couple of minutes and I can take you over to the cabin and show you around."

Slana Post Office

A few minutes later she was locking up the post office. She walked over to Mike and Casey and shook Casey's hand. "Hi, welcome to Slana. I'm Linda Jo, the only postal worker for miles around. Mike tells me you're interested in my little cabin on the river. You've come a long way!"

Casey smiled, instantly drawn to the woman. "Yes, and I only have a few days before I have to get back to the lower forty-eight."

Linda Jo smiled as she locked the door of the post office. "Let's not waste any time and head on over there."

They all piled into Mike's car and drove back onto the Tok Cutoff. After four miles he turned down a small gravel drive to the little half-built cabin on an acre of land that sat on the Slana River facing Wrangell-St. Elias Park.

The cabin was a one room, six hundred square feet, unfinished wood structure with a few small windows cut into the plywood. There was a roof and a floor, and other than a nice root cellar, that was it. The acre of land was level and covered with white birch, spruce, and willow trees. Fireweed and an assortment of berry bushes were sprinkled amongst the trees, and thick moss covered much of the ground. Several large trees along the bank of the river towered over the landscape. Casey pointed toward a place near the river. "That would be a nice area for a vegetable garden if I could clear some of these trees."

Casey's unfinished cabin

Casey saw that a well had already been dug and appeared to be functional. Linda Jo commented, "There's not much permafrost on the land, which means you can have a septic tank and have running water for bathroom facilities."

"Wait a minute," Casey said. "I need electricity to run the pump for that water."

Linda Jo smiled, "Yes, there would be a lot of things to figure out."

Casey began to make a mental note of all the questions she needed to ask Linda Jo. Finishing the cabin and getting things up and running would be a challenge, and no electricity would bring issues that she knew nothing about.

In spite of the obvious obstacles that would lie ahead for her, Casey loved the little cabin and the acre of land it sat on, although she did feel a little overwhelmed with all the new information she was trying to process.

Mike had a good suggestion. "Why don't we go up to Duffy's Roadhouse for a cup of coffee and sort out some of the questions that Casey probably has."

Linda Jo gave her a sympathetic look. "Great idea. Duffy's is only a mile up the road. We can sort out the entire list of questions that are probably swimming around in your head right now. If you want the place, we can figure out how to make it work for you."

Casey took Linda Jo's arm,. "Let's go. I'm ready to make this happen."

They climbed into the car and took off for Duffy's, the neighborhood roadhouse. Duffy's was an old log structure that leaned to one side. Casey learned later that Duffy's was built on perma frost, which made it shift from time to time when the frozen ice below would melt and refreeze. Casey looked around while cautiously stepping inside the building. A few old, dilapidated stools were pulled up to the bar, and three wooden tables crowded into the remaining space of the rooms. With only a couple of small windows, the room was fairly dark and dingy. Casey learned from Linda Jo that windows were usually built small to minimize the heat escaping during the bitter cold winter months, when temperatures were likely to plummet to -70. The three of them pulled out chairs and sat at one of the tables to have their coffee and mull over Casey's questions.

Casey explained to Linda Jo, "One of my main concerns about buying the cabin and property is all the work that would need to be done before I could move in. I'm still driving my big rig in the lower forty-eight. I need to be back on the road in just a couple of days. I want to buy the property, but I can't drive my truck and work on the cabin at the same time. And there's a lot of work to be done before I could move in."

Linda Jo had the answer. "Why not hire a couple of locals to do the work on the cabin until it's far enough along to where you can move in and finish the work yourself? Then you could quit your job, pack up your belongings and make the move up here.

Casey scratched her head. "It sounds like a good plan, but what locals are you talking about?"

Linda Jo thought for a minute. "I was thinking of Jonah Carlye. He lives out Nebesna Road, a place we call Four Mile. It's deeper in the bush, but it's accessible by car for most of the way, though he does like to drive his ATV. Jonah has done some trapping and has sold some of his furs in Anchorage. He is also handy with a hammer and has done a lot of carpenter work around Slana. His brother Billy Joe lives out at Four Mile too and often helps him with jobs. They did a good job when they built my cabin a few years back. Jonah also has experience as a plumber and has done some drywall work. People in these parts live and survive by doing a little bit of everything."

Casey was drawn to life in the bush. It was everything she had ever dreamed of, and she felt she was ready to start a new chapter in her life. Linda Jo offered to telephone Jonah that evening to see if he would meet with them tomorrow to discuss the work that needed to be done. Mike and Casey decided to drive back to Glennallen so Casey could check into the Caribou Hotel for the night. Later that evening, Mike called and said he had heard from Linda Jo. Jonah was interested in the job, and they were to meet them tomorrow at Duffy's Roadhouse at 11 a.m.

After a good night's sleep, Casey was up early and decided to have breakfast at the local café, called The Hitching Post. The townspeople seemed to be friendly and laid back. When the waitress brought Casey her coffee, sourdough pancakes and reindeer sausage she asked if she was new in town.

"Yes, I'm looking at some property in Slana. I'm planning on checking out the area today before I have to return to the lower forty-eight."

The waitress said, "Go by the Copper Basin Visitor Center and they'll give you information about subsistence permits. Most residents living in Slana live off the land as much as they can. I know they have a couple of fish wheels going when the salmon are running, and a few of the natives still fish with dip nets."

Casey thanked her for the information and decided not to linger over her breakfast. She wanted to go by the visitor center before it was time to meet Mike. The clerk at the visitor center gave her a lot of good information that would be helpful if she decided to move to the area. She also recommended that while Casey was in Slana, she should go by the Nebesna Ranger Station to learn more about the rules and regulations for hunting and fishing and subsistence living. It was a lot for Casey to think about. It would be a whole new way of life if she decided to make the move.

****

Mike and Casey met Linda Jo and Jonah at Duffy's Roadhouse at 11 a.m. Jonah, a tall, nice-looking man in his early fifties was able to answer most of Casey's questions. He understood her concerns about getting the cabin finished while she continued to drive long haul in the lower forty-eight. They agreed on a fair hourly wage for both Jonah and Billy Joe. There would also be a couple of trips to Anchorage for lumber and supplies. Casey was confident that Jonah and Billy Joe could do the job, and Jonah agreed to send pictures of the cabin while the work was being completed along with a tally of expenses and the weekly hours they worked. Casey felt comfortable with the construction plan that was agreed upon, and a contract was set up between them to have the cabin completed within three months. During that time she would be sending weekly checks for the work that was being done. Mike drew up another contract between Linda Jo and Casey to purchase the land and cabin for $40,000.

After what felt like a long day, they were on their way back to Glennallen. Casey planned on staying another night at the Caribou Hotel, so Linda Jo invited her back up to Slana the following day to see her cabin and some of Jonah's handy work. She also wanted to introduce her to some of the local residents. Casey asked if they could go by the Nebesna Ranger Station and maybe see the fish wheel.

Casey was at Linda Jo's cabin by 10 a.m. Linda Jo asked, "Do you want to stop by Midway, the local general store, and meet a few Slana residents? Midway has a little bit of everything. If Midway doesn't have what you're looking for, then your only other option is to make the trip into Glennallen or Tok, both about the same distance from Slana. Rule of thumb is, always check with your neighbor to see if they have what you need before you make the trip to town."

Casey was beginning to see how Slana was an interdependent little town, very different from what she was use to back home. Midway General Store did have a little bit of everything, from groceries to hardware, a few souvenirs, a couple of public showers, and two washers and dryers. There was even a computer that local residents could use for a fee of ten dollars a month. The computer helped keep local residents connected to the outside world.

"How do all these services work without electricity?" Casey asked.

"Midway has a large generator that runs twenty-four hours a day. It's the only place in Slana with round-the-clock electricity. Well, other than the elementary school—that runs off a generator too. Some day we might have electric along the Cutoff, but that is a whole other issue. A few of the locals are against it. They want to keep Slana as it has been for generations, a remote settlement in the wilderness." Casey tended to agree with those few locals.

As Linda Jo and Casey continued their conversation, a small, thin woman in her mid-thirties, dressed in jeans and a sweat shirt, approached them. "Hi, I'm Katy. Welcome to Slana. I've always got a fresh pot of coffee brewing. How about a cup? It's on the house."

Smelling the fresh brew, Casey replied, "Yes, that sounds good, thank you. Linda Jo has told me about your store and how everyone enjoys coming here, not just to get supplies but to catch up on the town gossip."

Katy laughed. "Yes, that's true. My husband and I bought Midway about ten years ago from another resident who still lives in the area. Other than Duffy's, it's the only other business around here. We serve the people who live in the surrounding area between Chistochina and Mentasta Lodge. We also get quite a few tourists coming into Alaska from Canada. They're usually on their way to Valdez or Anchorage."

After an hour of visiting with Katy and a few locals who dropped in for groceries and conversation, Linda Jo and Casey decided to go to the Nebesna Ranger Station to meet Bet, the ranger in charge. Bet was a friendly red-head in her mid-fifties, that Casey took a liking to right off. Bet gave Casey all the information she needed about becoming a resident of Alaska and living a subsistence lifestyle. A resident had to be living in the state for at least six months out of the year before they could qualify to hunt and fish with a subsistence permit. To use the fish wheel, Casey would need to register at the Ranger Station and report how many salmon she was taking from the wheel. Residents were allowed three hundred salmon a year.

Casey thought that was a lot of fish for just one person. "Why do they allow you to take so many fish?"

Bet replied, "Traditionally, a fish wheel could catch hundreds of fish when the salmon are running strong. Residents might be feeding their entire family for the year on the season's catch. Even though there is only one person in your family, you're allowed the same amount of fish. But be aware—we keep an eye on everyone who has a subsistence permit. You are not allowed to sell the fish; you can smoke them or can them, but it's a strict rule never to sell them." Casey thanked Bet for the information and she and Linda Jo left the Ranger Station.

Their last stop was the Copper River to see the fish wheel. It was pulled up out of the river, sitting on the side of the bank. When salmon season began in early June, a couple of the men would put the wheel in the water. The swift current of the Copper River would turn the paddle on the wheel, and the basket on the opposite side of the fish wheel would catch the salmon and dump them into the fish box. All a person had to do is pick them up out of the box and take them home to either eat or can. Of course, there isn't much sport to it, but people can always fish in the traditional way when they have enough time and enough food stored up for the winter. A whole different way of life.

Time flew by fast. It was already 3 p.m. and time to get back to Glennallen. Casey thanked Linda Jo for her hospitality and a wonderful day, and they agreed to keep in touch while Casey went back to driving over the road. Casey was hoping to make her move to Slana by September. That would give Jonah and Billy Joe the time they needed to make the cabin livable enough for her to move into. She wanted to be moved in before winter set in, which could be very soon in Alaska. Casey was now anxious to get back to the lower forty-eight. It was almost 5 p.m. when she arrived in Glennallen. As she headed toward the Caribou Motel, she saw Mike leaving his office. She pulled into the parking lot to say good-bye and to thank him for the extra effort and time he had put into the sale of her new home. They promised to keep in touch.

The trip back to Anchorage on the Glenn Highway was beautiful but uneventful. Her focus had shifted to everything she needed to do to prepare for her trip to Alaska and the long drive she would need to make up the Alaska Highway and to her little cabin in the wilderness.

Chapter Four: Getting Ready for the Journey North

As the aircraft landed on the runway of the Tacoma-Seattle airport, Casey looked out the window and saw an overcast day with a threat of rain in the air. She was glad to be on the ground. The five days she had spent in Alaska were a whirlwind, and she was exhausted from the trip. She picked up her luggage, hailed a cab, and within an hour she was at the drop yard where her tractor was waiting for her. Unfortunately, that was not all that was waiting for her. Mitch had learned from dispatch that Casey had taken her home time in Seattle instead of St. Louis, where she usually spent her days off.

Mitch walked over to her truck and banged on the driver's door. "Where have you been for the last four days? Even dispatch didn't know where you were. What are you trying to hide? Who are you sneaking around with?"

"Stop badgering me!" Casey yelled. "I don't need to give an account of where I've been to you or to dispatch. Get away from my truck before I call the guard at the gate."

"Bitch," Mitch muttered, but he stepped down from the step of Casey's truck.

She planned to avoid Mitch as much as possible, which was no easy feat since they ran the same routes. Casey had told no one where she had been or what her plans were of moving to Alaska. She needed to keep her plans a secret even when it was time to give her notice that she was quitting her job. She wanted no one but close family members to know what she was up to.

After Mitch finally left the drop yard to pick up his load, Casey decided to call her dispatcher to let him know that she would be ready for a load tomorrow. She curled back into her bunk that night with the pamphlets she received from the visitor center and the ranger station. Thoughts began to race through her head. *Am I really ready for this? Did I make this decision too quickly? Am I really up to the challenge of living in a remote wilderness area where temperatures are so extreme?* She knew she was running away from Mitch, but she also knew her lifelong dream was just waiting to happen.

She remembered back when she was in truck-driving school and how afraid she was to drive that big truck with all those gears. Laughing to herself, she also remembered the day she overcame her fears. She had previously gotten angry at another truck driver who was trying to push her out of her space in the fuel line by banging his truck up against hers, making it impossible for her to fuel her rig. She had been pushed around long enough, and from that point on she decided that fear was not her friend. She would take charge of her life and the challenging situations that seem to arise on a regular basis when driving an eighteen-wheeler. Would moving to Alaska be the same way? Would she gain the confidence she would need to take care of herself and live in rural Alaska? It was such a whole new world. She knew it would be one day at a time or sometimes one minute at a time, but she also knew that she could do it. She fell asleep with those thoughts tumbling through her mind.

Casey awakened the next morning with the buzzer on her truck computer blaring in her ear. It was her load information from dispatch.

She rolled out of her bunk, wondering where dispatch might be sending her this morning. After picking up her computer, she read that her load was at the Tacoma drop yard where she was already parked. The load was to be delivered to Hall Street drop yard in St. Louis in four days and in close proximity to where her two sons lived. If she could get her load delivered early enough, she might have time to meet her sons for breakfast and tell them of her news about moving to Alaska.

Before driving out of the drop yard with her load, she looked around for Mitch's truck, but he was nowhere in sight. She was hoping that he had not gotten a load that would be taking him in the same direction that she was traveling, east on Interstate 90. She wasn't as concerned during daylight hours when she could travel on a busy interstate. Casey mapped out a plan to take her ten-hour break at a busy Flying J truck stop along the Interstate. She could shower, have dinner, and hang out in the driver's lounge, where there were plenty of drivers. She even planned to park her truck in a lighted area near the main building where she knew security would be close by. She felt like she was being a little paranoid, but at the same time she wanted to feel safe.

Casey's day was uneventful as she drove along the interstate. The weather was sunny and no rain in sight. She needed an easy day of driving after her tiring trip to Alaska and back to the lower forty-eight in only five days.

There were so many things that needed to be done before she could make her trip up to Slana on the Alaska Highway. It was hard to keep her mind on her driving.

Her driving hours passed quickly. Casey pulled into a Flying J along the highway, looking forward to spending a quiet evening and hopefully getting another good night's sleep. She parked her truck for the night in a well-lit area and decided to go in and take a shower. As she walked into the driver's lounge to get her shower ticket, she spotted Mitch talking to another driver. Casey wanted to run, but she knew there was nowhere to go that was better than where she was parked for the night. She went about her business, took her shower, and returned to her truck for some quiet time.

Before long Mitch was banging on her driver's door again. Casey could hear her heart pounding as she peeked out her truck window. In a stern voice she demanded, "Leave me alone!" She lucked out. Mitch left without incident, muttering only a few choice words, but Casey knew he would be back when there were less people around. She stayed in her truck with the doors locked. Next she called her dispatcher and the safety department to report the harassment. The trucking company informed Casey that they sent Mitch a computer message telling him to stay away from her and not to approach her truck. The Safety Department also informed Casey that they were calling him into the terminal to discuss his behavior and that she needed to, again, make a formal complaint.

Casey didn't have much hope that any of their efforts to protect her from Mitch would do any good. She needed to protect herself. After dinner, when the security guards at Flying J came on for their night shift, she approached them and told one of the guards of her situation with Mitch and his ongoing harassment. The guard reassured Casey that they would keep an eye on him. There was no trouble with Mitch that night and Casey got a good night's sleep. She was up early the next morning and anxious to get back on the road and away from Mitch. The trucking company that Casey worked for must have called Mitch into the terminal to reprimand him for harassing her, because for the next two days she didn't see or hear from him.

Forty-eight hours later she pulled into the St. Louis drop yard. Her plan was to get a few hours of sleep and then meet with her sons over breakfast and give them her news about moving to Slana. Her boys were both grown and married with families of their own, but she wasn't sure how they would feel about her moving so far away and to such a remote area. They both knew of her lifelong dream of living in rural Alaska, so Casey hoped they would be supportive of the move.

Casey's sons arrived at the drop yard around 8 am and greeted their mom with a big bear hug.

"How's it going, Mom?" Bob, her oldest son, asked as they all walked across the street to the local café. "We didn't see you during your regular home time. What have you been up to?"

Casey cautiously looked up at her two sons and took a deep breath. There was no time like the present to tell them she was moving to Slana.

Bob and Mark knew something was up as they slid into a booth at the local restaurant. Casey smiled and said, "Well, I spent my home time in Slana, Alaska looking at a beautiful little piece of property with a half-built cabin on it. It's been a whirlwind of a weekend, but I did buy it and I plan to quit my job and move there as soon as I can."

She waited for their reaction. Bob and Mark's eyes were the size of saucers as they glared across the table at their mother.

Bob said, "What, I know you have always talked about moving to Alaska someday, but this is really sudden. Where is Slana, Alaska?

Casey answered, "My new home is in a very remote area in the interior of Alaska between two native villages along the Tok Cutoff. And there's no electricity."

Her oldest son Bob scratched his head. "Living in a remote wilderness area is one thing, but no electricity? Just how is that going to work?"

Mark looked at Bob over the breakfast menu. "Sounds good to me. We knew you were going to end up there someday anyhow.Right, Bob?" Mark laughed. "She might be our mom, but she's a grown woman who has been making her own decisions for some time now."

Bob looked irritated. "That's true, Mark, but that's a very harsh environment for a single woman in her mid-forties."

Casey frowned and was now clearly annoyed by her oldest son's remark but chose to disregard the condescending remark.

"She's been living in the cab of her truck for the past three years," Mark said, "and she's done all right for herself. It'll work out, Bob. If it doesn't, she'll be back."

Casey took another deep breath and interrupted their conversation "Slana is nestled right next to the Wrangell-St. Elias National Park and Preserve. The park borders my property. It's the largest park in the world and one of the wildest. Can you imagine yourself hunting there?"

Casey had checked the rules when she was at the Nebesna Ranger Station and learned that if her sons came to visit, they would need to purchase a non-resident hunting license; but they wouldn't need a professional guide as long as they were hunting with a blood relative.

Bob and Mark looked at each other and smiled. "This could work out real nice," Mark said.

Casey smiled. "I knew you'd like that. We could hunt together; think about it—bear, moose, caribou, mountain goats, Dall sheep. It's an opportunity of a lifetime."

After another hour of coffee and conversation, Bob was on board and they all agreed to go to Sikeston to buy a trailer for Casey's trip up the Alcan Highway. Her next home time would be in three weeks. Bob knew of a good dealer who sold trailers at a reasonable price; plus, Sikeston was the home of the renowned Lamberts roll-throwing restaurant. They would have a great time throwing rolls and buying a trailer for her trip north.

Casey said, "Well, I'm burnin' daylight. I need to get back on the road and pick up my next load." She was glad she had decided not to mention Mitch. She told her sons that she would see them in three weeks.

Back on the road again, Casey began to think about all of her future plans. She knew Jonah and Billy Joe were working hard to get her cabin ready. She started making a mental list of the things that she needed to do to get ready for her move north.

She had an old cab-over-camper that fit on the back of her one-ton

27

pickup truck that would serve her well on her trip up the Alaska Highway. Her one-ton would have no problem pulling a trailer with her belongings, and she could sleep in the camper wherever she decided to park for the night. The trailer would also be useful in Alaska when she would need to drive to Anchorage for supplies. Even though she knew Jonah and Billy Joe were doing much of the work, there would still be a lot more work that needed to be done once she arrived in Slana.

For the next few weeks Casey picked up and delivered loads and tried to keep her mind on her job while keeping her truck on the road. She saw Mitch a few times at truck stops along her route. His sarcastic remarks were nothing she couldn't handle, so she just tried to ignore him. She had more important things to occupy her mind. Casey made weekly phone calls to Jonah to check on the progress they were making on her cabin. Jonah had checked out the forty-foot well that had been previously dug by the original owner, and he thought it was a good well with no sign of permafrost, which meant Casey could have a septic tank for bathroom facilities. She liked the idea of living out in the wilderness with no electricity, and she was pleased to learn that she would be able to have a toilet that flushed and running water for a shower.

Jonah had reported that they had been to Anchorage to pick up the windows, a heat stove, kitchen and bathroom sinks, plus a toilet and shower stall. They were also able to fit on his trailer all the piping they needed to get the plumbing done. There was plenty to keep them busy for the next two or three weeks.

Casey's home time came and went. She enjoyed the time spent in St. Louis with her sons. They had a good time in Sikeston choosing a trailer and catching rolls at Lambert's Restaurant. Casey was used to visiting her family every month and would miss them after she moved, even though she knew they would be up for a visit. In three days her home time was up, and she needed to get back to driving her truck over the road.

While Casey was driving, Bob and Mark did electrical work on her trailer, hooking up the brake lights to her one-ton truck. Everything was getting done, and better yet, right on schedule. Casey heard from Jonah the following week. He and Billy Joe had made another trip into Anchorage for more supplies. This time they brought back all the insulation and the log siding that was needed for the cabin. Jonah estimated another month of work and the place would be ready for Casey to move in. There would still be much for Casey to do once she moved into her cabin. She told Jonah how much she appreciated him for all the work he and Billy Joe were putting into her cabin and for his commitment to continue to help her finish the work once she moved in.

When Casey decided to give an official two week notice that she was quitting her shop as a professional truck driver she knew it would get back to Mitch quickly but she was no longer afraid of him. She had told no one, other than her family, that she was leaving the area. Casey wanted to keep it that way, so she spread the rumor that she was moving back to St. Louis to look for a day job driving a truck. No one would be the wiser or expect anything different.

Chapter Five: Northbound on the Alaska Highway

Casey planned to give herself two weeks to drive from St. Louis, through Canada, and into Alaska. She had always heard of the wild life—bear, caribou, and even stone sheep could be seen in the Yukon Territory. Jonah had sent her The Mile Post, a step-by-step map that would lead her straight up the Alcan Highway right into Alaska. The Mile Post was a book that was great for pointing out camp sites, motels, and even restaurants along the way. Once she reached the Alaska border, Slana was only three hours away. Not getting ahead of herself, Casey was reminded that she had a lot work to do before she was ready for her trip north into Alaska.

After making a timeline in her mind, she decided it would take her a week to go through her storage bin and determine what she would need to take and what she would have to leave behind. Her cabin was only six hundred square feet, and there just wasn't room for everything she wanted to take. Her grandmother's antique hutch was a must. There is no way she could bear to part with it. The hutch could provide her with added kitchen space as well as countertop space for baking and preparing meals. When she reached her new home, she wouldn't have any cabinets and would have to make do until she knew what she needed or what she had room for. There were several boxes of clothes that she was not going to need. Ninety percent of those clothes were going to have to go, as well as all of those shoes. A few pair of jeans, some flannel shirts, and one pair of boots was all she decided to pack. Everything else was going to have to go.

Her tools were essential so she could continue the work on the cabin. Jonah had put in a kitchen sink and would have the water pumping from the well, but she would need cabinets and a countertop. Casey was planning on putting those in, and Jonah had offered to help if she needed it.

Her double bed and a dresser along with one comfortable living room chair would also go on the trailer. Pots and pans and dishes were also packed, along with bath towels and bedding. Casey wanted to take her battery inverter she used while driving her rig over the road. That would serve her well when she got to Alaska. She would be able to save electricity by using her inverter when her generator was not running. Casey was planning on buying a generator before she left the lower forty-eight so when she got to Slana, she could get it set up as soon as possible. She took a couple of oil lamps as well.

Basically, everything she needed for her first six weeks in Slana she packed into the trailer. That would give her a chance to settle into her cabin and determine what she needed before she needed to go to town for supplies. Winter could come quickly and unexpected, and she might have only a few short weeks before snow could fall and make travel to town more difficult.

Bob and Mark arrived early to help pack up the trailer and see their mother off. They worked together tying everything down with a tarp to protect Casey's belongings from bad weather as she drove up the Alaska Highway. Casey shed a few tears as he said goodbye to her two sons. It was hard to drive away..

Once Casey was on her way, driving west on Interstate 70, she wiped her eyes and began to feel better. Her truck was riding smooth, even with the overhead camper and the trailer attached. The one-ton pickup had no problem with the heavy load.

It was a beautiful August day, six o'clock in the morning, and the sun was rising in the sky over the trees along the highway. It felt good to leave the St. Louis rush hour traffic behind. Finally, she was on her way to Alaska, a dream coming true after all these years. It was really happening. She knew she had a hard road ahead, but what an adventure it would be. As she felt a warm breeze blowing through her hair, she said out loud, "Northbound into the wilderness—ready or not, here I come."

For the next couple of days, Casey thought about how nice it was to leave Mitch and trucking behind. She was looking forward to the new life ahead for her even though she knew there would be challenges ahead. The next couple of days brought good weather as the time flew by. She pulled into her last rest stop just north of Great Falls. Casey stopped early for the night to relax and to get a good night's sleep. Her plan was to stop off in Shelby and find a local bank to buy some Canadian dollars before she crossed the border into Canada.

Crossing the border into Canada was uneventful, but Casey was glad it was behind her, after hearing stories of people being detained for hours. She was relieved to have left the lower forty-eight and decided it was time to pull out The Mile Post, the travel authority for anyone traveling through Canada and into Alaska. According to the map, she would be traveling on the east access route all the way to Dawson Creek, BC, where she would eventually get on the Alaska Highway, which would take her into Alaska. Dawson Creek was a two-day drive, depending how often she wanted to stop. The road was well paved, the sky was clear and Casey intended to soak up the beautiful scenery along her route to Dawson. The next couple of days went by quickly after she decided to stay on the road and view the countryside from her truck. After driving through Calgary and avoiding rush-hour traffic, she continued north until she came to a campground near the town of Red Deer. It was one of the campgrounds recommended in The Mile Post.

Casey pulled into the campground at 8:30 p.m. After parking her truck next to a grove of trees, she could hear water washing along the rocks of a creek bed. She glanced across the road and spotted a few campers sitting around a fire, enjoying each other's company. She decided to walk over to their campsite and introduce herself. Even with the warmth of their campfire, there was a cool breeze blowing, and the cup of hot chocolate they offered Casey was appreciated.

She sat down on a nearby campstool and introduced herself. "I'm Casey, I've been travelling north for the past couple of days, and I'm moving to Slana, a small settlement in the interior of Alaska."

"We're from Fairbanks," an elderly man answered. "My wife and I will be visiting family in the lower forty-eight." The man gave Casey an odd look and said "I'm familiar with the small town of Slana. It's in a very remote part of Alaska. No electricity..You're going up there by yourself?"

"Yes, I am. It's been a dream of mine since I was a young girl." Casey really didn't want to have a discussion about a single woman moving to a rural area all by herself. Trying to change the subject, she asked the couple, "This is the first time I have traveled through Canada. Since you are traveling south, what kind of scenery and wild life have you seen on your trip so far?"

Stone Sheep getting nutrients from the rocks

His wife, getting the message, answered. "Yes, we came through some beautiful country, and the wild life in the Yukon is awesome. We saw mostly black bears and a couple of grizzlies—we could see them right from our car. We also saw stone sheep on the rocky hillsides of the mountains in the Yukon Territory. They came right down on the road next to our car."

The man from Fairbanks added, "The road is curvy and you really need to slow down and watch where you are going. Don't let the sheep distract you."

Casey smiled. "I won't, and I'll be careful too!"

They visited for another hour, enjoying each other's stories along with their hot chocolate, until it was time for Casey to say good-night. Morning would come soon enough and she wanted to get an early start. If road conditions were good and the weather was in her favor, her plan was to get to Dawson Creek by tomorrow night.

Once Casey passed Edmonton, the road to Dawson Creek was cluttered with a lot of construction and frequent gravel breaks, plus a washed-out bridge that caused a delay of over an hour. At one point Casey pulled over to check The Mile Post to see how far the drive was to Dawson. She decided to just keep going since the weather was good and there would be plenty of daylight for several hours. She passed the town of Whitecourt and found the road to have fewer gravel breaks, but the dust was bad due to lack of rain in the area. She continued to drive through Valleyview, then Grande Prairie, looking forward to when she could stop for the night. Just north of Dawson Creek she found a campground with several paved parking spots and both a shower house and a small grocery store on the premises, which was all she needed to stop for the night. A hot shower and a cup of chamomile tea and she was asleep, dead to the world. Daylight came early the next morning, with the sun peering through the camper blinds. In less than twenty minutes, Casey was up and dressed and walking over to the small grocery store for a coffee and bagel, then she was back on the road. Long hours and little sleep was something Casey was accustomed to from driving her rig cross country. She was looking forward to leaving those days and memories behind her.

After checking The Mile Post one more time, she reassured herself that she could make it to Muncho Lake by nightfall. The campers from Red Deer had told her that Strawberry Flats Campground was a good place to stay. The campground was located on the rocky lakeshore of Muncho Lake. The Mile Post described the lake as a beautiful seven-mile scenic lake with striking green and blue waters. After she reached the campground, her plan was to stay for a couple of days while she visited Liard Hot Springs, a few miles north of the lake.

The road ahead had a lot of frost heaves due to high elevations. Casey drove through curvy, winding roads along the mountain passes while stopping at a few turnouts to admire the beautiful rocky terrain that reaches towards the clouds. A small family of stone sheep high along the rocky hillside could be seen from the road, but Casey knew it wasn't safe to stop so she cautiously took pictures from her truck as she drove towards the lake.

As Casey drove over Summit Peak she could view the lake to the left of her. She knew Muncho Lake would not be far ahead so she reluctantly drove on, passing one of the turnouts for picture taking. She knew she had a couple of days to relax and enjoy Muncho Lake and Liard Hot Springs. She was interested in getting to Strawberry Flats Campground as soon as possible.

It was worth the long hours of driving to reach the lake by nightfall. She found an ideal place to park her truck and trailer, beneath a grove of trees facing the lake. When she woke the next morning she was facing a picture perfect view of the serene lake. After coffee and a hot breakfast, she decided to take a leisurely walk along the lakeside trail, savoring the scents of the fresh, clean air.

By mid-morning she returned to her campsite and unhooked the trailer so she could drive up to Liard Hot Springs. She parked her truck and began walking along the boardwalk trail. She enjoyed the beauty of the wetlands that supported several boreal forest plants, including several different species of orchids that were native to the natural wetlands due to the hot springs. It was a little piece of heaven, although a few signs warned her to be on the lookout for moose and bear in the area. Casey spent three hours soaking in the hot springs before she decided it was time to go back to the campground at Muncho Lake. It had been a wonderful day, and Liard Hot Springs was exactly what she needed to help her relax and unwind. Casey got up early the next morning to watch the sunrise and decided to take another walk on the lake trail before she got back on the road again. She had one more stop that she wanted to make before she got to Alaska, and that was Watson Lake, known as The Gateway to the Yukon. At the north end of town she planned to make a short stop at the famous Sign Post Forest where travelers are encouraged to leave a sign while passing through. As of September, 2000 there had been more that 43,000 signs added to the Sign Post Forest. Back in the lower forty-eight before she left on her trip north, she had read in the Milepost about the Sign Post Forest, so she brought an old street sign that she had from when she was a child. The sign read Hilldale Avenue, which was the name of the street she lived on when she was a young girl and where her dream of living in the wilderness of Alaska was born. Tears came to Casey eyes as she nailed her street sign to one of the posts. She thought to herself, *Dreams do come true If you have the courage and determination to make them happen.* She walked through the signpost forest looking at all the signs and knew there was a story behind every sign there.

Sign Post Forest
Courtesy of Creative Commons Attribution-Share Alike and Wikipedia Commons

A couple of hours later Casey left the Sign Post Forest, heading down the road toward Teslin, following the Rancheria River and driving over the Continental Divide. She saw mountain valleys that were lush with shades of green foliage as she continued to drive along the Swift River for several miles. It was a long day of driving and she ran into more frost heaves, which allowed her to slow down and enjoy the wildlife and spectacular scenery. After spending a long day on the road, she pulled into Mukluk Annie's R.V. for the night. Casey was just in time to have a home-cooked salmon dinner at Mukluk Annie's Restaurant, which was highly recommended in The Milepost.

Morning came early, with Casey leaving the R.V. park by 7 a.m. A cool breeze was blowing and the gray sky was threatening to snow. It was to be another long day on the road, and hopefully not another day of dodging the frost heaves in the road. If all went well she would be in Tok, Alaska by nightfall. Casey made only two stops, one at Haines Junction to fuel the truck and to grab a tuna salad sandwich for the road. The second stop was for a herd of caribou that decided to cross the road. She watched them as they traveled alongside her truck for over a mile.

She was getting close to the Alaska/Canadian border with less than ten miles to go. As she approached the border, she came to Port Alcan, U.S. Customs and Immigration Services, where officers were stopping vehicles, asking people if they were bringing any fruits or plants into Alaska. After being cleared, she drove across the state line, feeling a warm sensation while a few tears came to her eyes. It was an emotional moment for Casey to realize she had finally made it. She could truly say that she was on her way home.

Chapter Six: New Home in the Wilderness

Once Casey crossed the border, she felt a sense of relief. Canada and the Yukon Territory were as wild and stunning as she had always heard, but she was glad to be back on American soil. It was early evening when she drove into the town of Tok. As much as she wanted to drive into Slana, she knew it was best to stay at the R.V. park in town. She still needed to pick up her two firearms that she had previously sent to the gun shop in town. Spending the night in Tok would also allow her to pick up a few groceries and supplies in the morning.

As she drove down Main Street, she spotted the Sour Dough R.V. Park in the middle of town, located next to the Tok Visitor Center. Casey picked out a nice campsite with shaded spruce and white birch trees. After pulling into her spot and dropping her trailer she walked over to the visitor center and was greeted by a tall, husky woman. "May I help you?" the woman asked in a curt voice

"Yes, I just arrived in Alaska from the lower forty-eight," Casey answered. "I bought a cabin in Slana at milepost 66 on the Tok Cutoff. Can you tell me where the turnoff is?"

"About a half-mile down the road," the woman replied. "You can't miss it."

After looking around the visitor center and picking up some pamphlets on the area, Casey decided to drive around town to see what Tok had to offer. Tok, population 273, would be the closest town to Slana and where Casey planned to pick up most of the groceries and supplies that she would need. When she drove down Main Street she saw Grizzly's Hardware Store, Three Bears Grocery Store, and the gun shop. In the morning she would need to stop at all three places before she drove to Slana. Driving back to her campsite, she thought it would be a good idea to call Jonah to see if he could meet her in the morning to help her unpack her trailer. She also wanted him to check out the generator she had bought in the lower forty-eight. There was going to be a lot for Casey to learn, and she was grateful for Jonah's help. Her move to Alaska could have never happened without Jonah and Billy Joe. She was beginning to understand that living out in the bush meant that she would be part of an interdependent community. People living in Slana understood that it was a matter of survival that made their unique lifestyle possible. After living in the city her whole life, she wondered if the adjustment would be a difficult one for her to make.

Jonah answered his phone on the first ring and was happy to hear that Casey had made it through Canada without any mishaps. "Glad you made it to Tok, and in record time, I might add. Not bad for a city girl."

"City girl." Casey chuckled. "Don't you mean 'a wanna-be bush woman'? I left the city girl back in St. Louis." Casey knew she was going to have to prove herself, and hopefully she was up to the task. She could only imagine the hard times that might be ahead for her. She figured she would need to develop a sense of humor and maybe grow another layer of tough skin. Driving long haul as a solo female driver was challenging, at best, but she was able to overcome the obstacles and eventually became comfortable as a long-haul truck driver. She knew she would rise to the challenge of living out in the wilderness as a single woman.

Morning came early in Tok, Alaska, with campers packing up and pulling out to get an early start for Anchorage or Fairbanks; both destinations were a five-hour drive through the mountains. She was meeting Jonah in the mid-morning at her cabin, so there was plenty of time to get her errands finished and to have a pleasant drive down the Tok Cutoff toward her new home. Casey knew her cabin was located at mile 66 about an hour and a half from town. "Home." She couldn't believe it. After coming so far then picking up a few supplies, she would start down the Cutoff on her last leg of her long journey up the Alaska Highway. It seemed surreal to Casey. As she turned onto the road leading to her new home and a whole new way of life, tears clouded her eyes as she thought of all the years she'd yearned to make her journey north into Alaska.

The surrounding mountain peaks were rocky and steep, seeming to touch the clouds with their jagged edges. Below the tree line grew tundra of bright yellow and brown hues. Short, scraggly spruce trees grew out of the soft ground where permafrost was present. Willows and white birch grew along the edges of small potholes of water. Bright purple wildflowers could be seen growing along the roadside as Casey continued her drive along the Tok Cutoff.

Casey noticed a huge bull moose at Milepost 86 and decided to pull over onto a gravel turnout to get a better look. The moose was standing in a nearby water hole dunking his huge head under the water and pulling up mouthfuls of grassy weeds. She had heard in the past that moose could be very unpredictable, so she thought it best not to get out of her truck. Watching safely from her vehicle, she sat quietly and snapped a few pictures while she watched him feed. He looked up at her several times but was not bothered by her presence. After the moose had his fill, he just walked off and disappeared into the nearby brush. What a sight it was for her to watch a moose feed in his natural habitat.

Along the same stretch of highway she was able to view several kinds of water fowl in the nearby ponds, including graceful trumpeter swans with their young. What a perfect spot for any wildlife photographer. She made a mental note in her mind—this was a place she wanted to come back to for a couple of hours to take pictures and view the water fowl.

Pulling back onto the road, she continued to drive, watching the mile markers so she wouldn't pass the driveway leading to her cabin. Within ten minutes she spotted a cardboard sign that read "The Huntley Cabin" with an arrow pointed at the driveway leading down to her cabin. Making a left turn into the drive, she could see Jonah, Billy Joe, and Linda Jo standing on the front porch, ready to greet her as she pulled up and parked her truck and trailer. *What a relief to finally make it home*, she thought.

Jonah was anxious to show Casey all the progress that had been done on the cabin. The log siding was perfect and exactly what Casey had pictured it to be. An arctic porch to keep the frigid air out of the cabin had been completed as well and a deck that reached out along the river side of the cabin. The bathroom was complete, with all the fixtures and amenities in place.

"What a job that was!" Jonah said with a sense of relief. "We had to insulate the pipes and bury them ten feet under the ground so the frost wouldn't freeze them up. We were able to get the septic tank in too. You were lucky we didn't hit permafrost, or you'd be using an outhouse like most folks do around here."

Casey smiled. "I'm grateful for the hard work you and Billy Joe put into my place, and even more grateful that I'll have running water and a toilet that flushes." Casey let out a laugh. "We city women do like those little extras that make life just a little more comfortable."

Jonah smiled back. "I know, I get it. But you need to understand that life out here in the bush needs to be kept as simple as possible. Things that work in the city don't work too well out here. Like that stupid electric coffee pot and waffle maker that you have packed over in that box on the floor. Those need to go! Your generator is only going to put out so much electricity, and you don't want to overload the circuit with things you don't need. I'm serious, Casey, these things are important."

Casey knew he was right, but she didn't like it one bit. There were so many things she never thought of, and so many things she knew she had to learn.

"I know you're right, Jonah," she said, "and I know I need to learn all these things, but all I can think of right now is, I finally made it to my dream of living in Alaska, in my little cabin where things are wild and free."

"Speaking of wild and free," Billy Joe chimed in, "I almost forgot to mention, you have a cow moose bedded down amongst those willows about two hundred yards from your front door. She gave birth to twin calves only four days ago. Whatever you do, don't step between that cow and her newborn calves. It's good to get in the habit of taking a good look in all directions when you step outside that door."

Very good advice, indeed., she thought. It was starting to dawn on Casey that she needed to have a little more respect for the dangers that existed in her new surroundings that she would now call home.

Billy Joe added, "Being cautious when working on the cabin or using power tools is another good idea. The closest doctor is in Gennallen, and if you get hurt bad, you could die before we could get you there. Anchorage is our closest hospital and it's five hours from here."

"I guess we're on our own out here," Casey said, realizing how isolated

41

she really was.

"Yes, you might say that," Jonah said, "but on the bright side, we do have Jesse, a family practitioner, who has a small log cabin for an office about fifteen minutes down the road from here. Jesse does a lot of preventive medicine and treats patients when they get hurt or sick. We're lucky to have her way out here."

Family practitioner's office fifteen miles from Slana

That was good news to hear. "I'm looking forward to meeting her and everyone else who lives in the area."

"Well we better help get your trailer unpacked, so you can get settled in," Jonah said. "I also want to show you the generator shed I built while you were driving up here. It's out back, about a hundred yards from the cabin, just in case your generator overheats; if it catches on fire, it won't burn down your cabin. I can help you get it set up tomorrow if you want me to come by."

Casey smiled. "Thanks, Jonah, that sounds good to me." It suddenly dawned on Casey that there wasn't a fire department nearby, or for that matter any police department either. She remembered what Mike had told her, that the villages of Chistochina and Mentasta had tribal police but Slana was unincorporated and under the protection of the state troopers, who were in Glennallen, an hour and a half away. Reality was beginning to set in. She felt overwhelmed with everything that she was trying to take in and everything that she knew she needed to know but hadn't learned yet. She was going to have to take one day at a time.

Thirty minutes later they had the trailer unloaded and what little furniture Casey brought with her inside the cabin, along with boxes that needed to be unpacked. She decided that it would be more comfortable to sleep in the cabin, but for meals and bathing she would use her camper until she had everything hooked up to the generator. That would probably take a couple of days.

By mid-afternoon everyone had left and she was alone in her new home. Casey sat back in her one and only chair, looking out the picture window, imagining the garden she planned to put in next spring. The ground between the cabin and the river was the perfect place. Before she could rototill the land, a few trees needed to come down so their root systems would not erode the river bank. Casey figured this fall would be the best time to take care of that, although she knew a lot needed to get done before she could think about that. Winter was right around the corner. It was late August already. She was grateful that Jonah was coming over tomorrow to work on getting the generator set up. The first thing on her agenda would be to call the gas company in Glennallen and have them deliver a propane tank and hook it up to the pipes in the cabin that Jonah had installed. That would allow Casey to run her propane refrigerator and stove. She also had a backup propane heater that would heat the cabin if she didn't want to use her wood stove. He would need two more tanks put in, one that would hold regular gas for her pickup truck and the second tank to hold diesel fuel to run the generator. The closest gas stations were in either Glennallen or Tok, and that drive was over an hour; too far to be traveling in the dead of winter just to fill up your tank.

After another thirty minutes of daydreaming and wondering what she was forgetting to do, she decided to get up out of her chair and unpack some boxes. While organizing what few clothes she brought with her and putting them into her dresser drawer, she realized that she needed more room for the winter extreme clothes and bunny boots that were a necessity for the winter months ahead. A few wooden pegs on the arctic porch would work well for coats. A large wooden box with a lid could serve as a bench to sit on as well as the storage space she would need for her boots and winter gear; she could build that herself without the help of Jonah or Billy Joe.

Casey's setup when she first moved into her cabin

It was early evening, almost time for dinner, so she walked out the door toward her camper, remembering to look both ways to make certain that cow moose was not around. "All clear" so she cautiously walked over to her camper to start dinner. It was evening when she started back to her cabin, looking around for the cow moose and seeing no sign of the animal or her twin calves. Casey knew that developing an awareness of her surroundings would eventually become second nature to her. After unpacking a couple more boxes, arranging the linens and sheets, she decided to make up her bed and retire for the night.

Casey's eyes popped open. It was 2 a.m, and she definitely heard a noise outside. Something was wrestling in the brush right outside her window. With her heart racing, she jumped out of bed and grabbed her rifle, which was hanging over the cabin door, and cautiously peeked out the window. It was the cow moose and her baby calves. They were right outside her window, only four feet away. The cow moose had a mouth full of willow branches and was bending them over where her baby calves could reach them. She was teaching them how to eat the willows that were all around her cabin. Casey snuck back slowly from the window and returned with her camera. She watched and took pictures of the moose and her calves for the next hour, then returned to bed knowing they were right outside her bedroom window. It was hard for Casey to fall back to sleep, but she needed to at least try; tomorrow was going to bring a long work day.

Chapter Seven: Meeting Neighbors

Morning brought a cool breeze blowing off the river. Casey had left her bedroom window open during the night in case the cow moose decided to come back for a visit. After glancing at the clock, which read 7 a.m, she decided to get up and make breakfast. In a couple of hours Jonah would be laying the pipes for the generator, and she wanted to be prepared to put in a good day's work. While watching out for the cow moose and her two calves, she decided to wander over to her camper to put on a pot of coffee and cook up a ham and cheese omelet. Casey figured that eating a hearty breakfast would give her a good start for a long day of hard work.

Jonah was soon knocking at her door, ready to go to work. "Are you ready to start digging trenches for the piping?" he asked with a smile on his face.

"I sure am." Casey smiled right back at him. "I'm ready to have my electricity as soon as possible, but don't you want to hear about that cow moose who came for a visit last night?"

"Oh my god, what happened, did she give you trouble?" Jonah's smile turned to a serious frown.

"Of course not," Casey answered. "I kept my distance and watched her feed her calves from the window. She was teaching them how to eat the willows. I got some great pictures."

Jonah smiled with a sigh of relief. "You're going to see a lot of wild animals out here. You're in their natural habitat. Just remember to give them plenty of space and don't startle them if you can help it, and always take your gun or rifle when you're out in the woods."

Moose close to Casey's cabin

Moose along the Tok Cutoff

Jonah always seemed to be giving Casey advice. She resented it, but she also knew she needed to hear it. Casey was very independent and use to taking care of herself in the lower forty-eight, but living out in the wilderness was a whole new experience. It was going to be a trial and error process, but she was looking forward to it.

Casey and Jonah went to work marking off where the trenches were to be dug. The work was hard but satisfying. Casey had never really thought about how electricity worked or what you had to do to get electricity in your home. It was always just there. She wondered how many other things she just took for granted.

After a few hours Jonah and Casey took a welcomed break and sat on the bank of the river with a cup of hot coffee. She could only imagine what the river would look like this winter when it was iced over. "When does the river ice up enough to where I can walk across to the other side?"

"I wouldn't chance it till the end of December or maybe January. The middle of the river is safe to travel on, but there are a couple of underwater springs along the bank where you could go through the ice and the river current would pull you under. It's best not to even try crossing at any time. You have no reason to cross that river."

Casey bit her tongue and thought to herself, *There he goes again, telling me what to do*. She knew it was good advice and she did need to know what the dangers were that seemed to lurk around every corner. Realizing that it was her own lack of knowledge that she resented, not Jonah—he was only trying to help—she decided to ease up on him.

In the distance, Casey heard the faint rumble of a motor boat. The sound grew louder and a flat-bottom boat appeared in front of them. In the boat was a man and a woman with what appeared to be a dead porcupine.

The man yelled out to Jonah as he swung the corpse in the air. "Good meat for dinner tonight! Is that the Cheechako that moved up here from the lower forty-eight?"

Casey took an instant dislike to that man but decided to keep her mouth shut. The woman with him was timid and said nothing as she tied his boat to the willow branches growing along the river bank. The man was middle-aged and overweight, with a long, gruff beard, dressed in tattered clothes with his pants held up by worn suspenders.

He stated in a brusque voice, "They call me Maxx and this is my missus, Anna." Anna nodded her head in acknowledgement but said nothing.

"Hi Anna, it's nice to meet you, and you too, Maxx," Casey said. "Jonah tells me you live just up the river from my place."

Anna, a lean, dark-haired woman dressed in jeans and a flannel shirt, said, "We've been out checking on some berry patches and thought we'd drop by to meet you. The word is out at Midway that you arrived yesterday. Did you have a good trip on your way up from outside?"

"Yes, I did," Casey replied. "Why don't you come up to my cabin and I'll show you around." Anna and Casey walked up from the bank and over to the cabin, leaving Jonah and Maxx down by the river.

"What kind of berries were you picking?" Casey asked.

"We were checking on a blueberry patch across the river about a mile downstream, but it's a little early and they're not quite ripe yet. I can tell by their size that it's going to be a good year for blueberries."

"What other kind of berries can you pick around here?"

"Other than blueberries, cranberries and raspberries are the most popular," Anna said, "but there are salmon berries and a few others that people eat around here. We also use the petals from the fireweed plant and rosehips from the wild rose plant to make jelly as well as the berries. The land provides us with just about everything we need. Maybe we can go berry picking sometime. I can show you where some good berry patches are."

Casey was excited about making a new friend. "I think that would be great."

Casey overlooking pipes leading into her cabin

Next thing Casey heard was Maxx yelling, "You need to get down here, Anna, let these people get back to work." They exchanged phone numbers while Anna scurried down the bank toward their boat.

Jonah and Casey went back to work digging out the trenches for the generator pipes. An hour passed when the gas man arrived from Glennallen with two fifty-gallon tanks, one tank for the propane that Casey needed for her refrigerator, gas cook stove, and her backup propane heater, and the other for the unleaded gas that she needed to fuel her truck with. The fuel was scheduled to be delivered tomorrow. It took the gas man about an hour to hook up the propane tank and set up the unleaded tank. Everything was going as scheduled and Casey was happy with all the progress that was being made.

It was late afternoon when they finished digging the trenches and decided to call it a day. While preparing a chicken sandwich and glass of tea, she decided that tomorrow would come soon enough. An evening off to sit out on the deck, enjoying the river along with her dinner, sounded relaxing. Since it became quiet when everyone left, she thought the cow moose and her calves might show up for a visit. No moose in sight, but a nice, cool breeze blew in over the river and rustled through the spruce trees. She was enjoying her chicken sandwich when the camp robbers showed up and perched on the deck, begging for her dinner. They were also perched in the willow and white birch trees that lined up along the river bank. If there was one there were twenty, all begging for her chicken sandwich. She threw them a few crumbs and knew they would probably eat from her hand with a little coaxing. She noticed that there were a lot of birds around that were native to Alaska that she was not yet familiar with. Casey loved birds and decided that she would make a bird feeder for them tomorrow. She was already planning on building the storage bench and wall pegs for her arctic room while Jonah was laying pipe and hooking up the generator. If the fuel came tomorrow, she would be ready to move into her cabin permanently. What a nice thought that was.

While relaxing, just finishing her sandwich, she heard the sound of an ATV motor. It sounded like it was coming down her driveway. She looked up and saw a man and woman in their late forties riding a four-wheeler. The man was tall, with curly black hair and a full beard. The woman with him was of medium height, with strawberry blonde hair that came down to her shoulders.

The man called out, "I'm Jed and this is my wife Robyn. We heard you moved in yesterday, so we thought we'd come by and introduce ourselves. We took the back trail through the woods to get to your place. We live over on Nebesna Road, just down from the ranger station."

Casey introduces herself and asked the couple to stay and visit for a spell. "Would you like a glass of tea?" They hopped off their four-wheeler and came up the steps to the cabin while Casey poured them each a tall glass of tea. It was nice to know that she had friendly neighbors. Robyn told Casey that she was a teacher at Slana Elementary School. There were only a handful of students living in the surrounding area, so she taught all the elementary grades in only two classrooms. Older students living along the Tok Cutoff were bussed into Glennallen to the high school or were home schooled by their parents. Jed was retired and did odd jobs for people around Slana. He offered to help with any work she might need done on her cabin.

Casey replied immediately, "I need to cut down around twenty trees, several along the river bank and a few around the cabin. And I want to put a garden in next spring." They all walked around the property with their glasses of tea deciding which ones would be the best to take out. Casey also planned to keep much of the wood to burn in her stove during the winter months.

Looking around the property, Jed said, "That's a good idea. If those trees along the river bank don't come down, they'll start to erode the soil between the cabin and the river and you'll lose part of your garden area."

"Why don't you come over to our place tomorrow?" Robyn said."We can show you how we cleared our land and put a garden in."

"I would love to," Casey replied. "Jonah is coming in the morning to finish up the hook-up for my generator, but afternoon would be good. How do I find your place?"

Robyn pointed to the driveway. "Make a left out of your driveway and take the Cutoff about five miles, then make a left on Nebesna Road. We're a half-mile on the left. It's a two-story log house with a gravel circle drive. How about late afternoon or whenever you finish up the work you need to get done while Jonah is at your place?" She smiled. "We Alaskans don't keep time schedules too good."

"Great, I'll be there as soon as I can get away from here," Casey said. Jed and Robyn said their good-byes and left on their four wheeler, waving as they drove toward the trail that led to their home.

Sitting back in her easy chair, Casey relaxed for another hour. It was a good way to end the day. She was a little disappointed that the cow moose didn't come out of the woods to feed on the nearby willows, but she wasn't really surprised. There was just too much noise and activity going on all day for her to show up with her calves. After unpacking a couple more boxes, she decided to call it an early night and went to bed. After a hard day's work, she had no trouble falling asleep, even though it was light outside. The twenty-four hours of daylight during the summer months did not seem to bother her. If that mama moose showed up, she was going to be too tired to even wake up to see her. As she closed her eyes, she reassured herself that there would be plenty of opportunity to see all the wild life she wanted to see.

Casey was up early and had already had her breakfast when Jonah came knocking on the door at 9 a.m. She invited him in to have a cup of coffee before he started working on the generator pipes. Jonah took her up on that cup of coffee and commented that it would only take him a couple of hours to get the pipes hooked up. As soon as they delivered the fuel, she would have electricity.

Casey grinned. "You've done a fine job in getting this place up and running in just a few short days. By the end of the day I will have my refrigerator full, my stove working, the water running, and the toilet flushing."

Jonah laughed, "The place is really looking good, although it may be a little expensive to run that generator all the time, but with a battery invertor you can store up some electricity for when you need it and save on the diesel fuel."

Casey had already thought of the cost of diesel fuel and knew she could only afford to run her generator a few hours a day, most likely in the evening when the need was greatest to run water and use lights. She would need to work up a schedule for her generator time. She could shower, do laundry, and wash the dishes in the evening. She had already rigged up a bucket with a lid for the bathroom. An attractive water pitcher sat on top of the bucket for flushing the toilet during the day. Every evening she planned to fill up three five-gallon buckets of water that she could use during the day when she was not able to pump the water from the well. Oil lamps could also be used in the day for light. She would be able to manage nicely. It was amazing to Casey how much she had taken for granted when she lived in the lower forty-eight. It gave her a good feeling to be self-sufficient.

Jonah went to work on getting the generator hooked up while Casey got started on building her storage bench for the arctic porch. The fuel trucks came to deliver the diesel and unleaded fuel, and everything got hooked up and was running the way it was supposed to. What an accomplishment that was. Before Jonah left he showed Casey how the electric panel worked and the do's and don'ts to keep the generator operating safely and efficiently. It was nice to completely move into the cabin and clean the camper up to be used for storage and future trips into Anchorage.

Chapter Eight: Meat for the winter

It was mid-afternoon when Casey was able to leave for Jed and Robyn's home. This was the first time she had been out and away from her cabin, and she was looking forward to visiting with her new neighbors. As she drove along the Cutoff, she passed Midway on the right, and about a half-mile further she made a left turn onto Nebesna Road. As Casey turned into Jed and Robyn's driveway, she saw a two-story log house with a pair of snow shoes nailed to the logs on their front porch. Beautiful white daisies lined the front of their home. To the left was a two-car garage that Jed used as a work shop to work on his many projects throughout the year. To the right on the other side of the log home was a large, screened-in porch that faced their greenhouse and vegetable garden. Their home was moderate and equipped with everything they needed to live comfortably out in the bush.

After a quick tour of the house Casey asked Robyn if she could see her greenhouse and garden area. Jed had built the little hothouse where they were growing tomatoes, peppers, cucumbers, and green beans. Jed was in charge of the greenhouse and insisted on caring for his tomatoes, which were eventually made into a pasta sauce and salsa from an old family recipe that had been handed down over the years.

Casey asked, "What kind of vegetables do you grow out in your garden?"

Robyn answered with a touch of pride in her voice, "Cold-weather plants, like broccoli, cauliflower, carrots, and onions. Lettuce and cabbage grow well, and I always plant a few rows of potatoes. It's a lot of work, but I love it. Do you know what you want to plant in your garden next year?"

Casey smiled. "I think I want to plant the same vegetables that you have, but the greenhouse I will wait on. I do want more rows of potatoes."

Jed joined the women as they were walking over to the garden. "What do you think of my green house?"

"It's beautiful," Casey answered. "I can see how it might keep you pretty busy. It must give you so much satisfaction to be able to grow and prepare your own food."

"Yes, it really does," Jed replied. "I usually wait to get my seedlings in by the middle of June after I'm sure the last freeze has taken place. I start my seedlings in the greenhouse by early May and transplant them out in the garden, which gives them a nice head start. Things grow fast up here with twenty-four hours of sunlight. By the end of August you need to have your garden harvested before winter sets in again."

It was exciting for Casey to see how equipped and efficient people could live in such a remote rural area with bitter cold temperatures during the winter months and such a short growing season during the summer months. She was looking forward to having her own garden by next spring.

They ventured into the garden and picked some lettuce leaves, a head of cabbage, a cucumber and a couple of tomatoes from the hothouse and packed them into a paper bag that Robyn pulled from her pocket. "Welcome to the neighborhood," she stated as she handed Casey the sack of produce.

Casey thanked her. "This will make a really nice salad for my dinner tonight."

"Sure will," Robyn said. "This is the only time of the year that we can get fresh produce. You can get some from Glennallen or Tok, but it's not fresh or homegrown. Soon I'll be picking the garden and greenhouse clean and canning what I can for the winter months. It's a big job."

Casey had a great idea. "I could help you. You would be doing me a favor, because next year I'll have my own garden and will need to learn all the do's and don'ts of canning."

Jed broke in at that moment with another great idea. "You need to take out those twenty-seven trees, and I could use four or five of the large ones to put around my driveway. We could get Maxx to haul them over here with his big rig. How about me helping Jonah take out those trees in exchange for you helping Robyn clean out the garden and do some canning?" He smiled. "As long as you don't mess up my salsa and pasta sauce."

"We won't," Robyn and Casey shouted at the same time. It was a wonderful idea. Casey could do some canning and get some hands-on training for winter food preparation. Best of all, she could get out of bringing down those trees, which she was not looking forward to. Casey was happy to be spending some time with her new friend, Robyn.

As Casey waved good-bye to Jed and Robyn, she climbed into her truck with her fresh bag of produce and thought to herself, *I just had my first lesson in bartering, and I must say, I got the better of the deal; at least from my perspective.*

****

It was the third week in August and Casey had met a few more neighbors, all of them friendly and ready to help in any way they could. Slana was a great place to live where everyone looked out for each other, and where sharing whatever you had was the norm, not the exception.

Anna had called earlier in the week and asked Casey if she wanted to drive to Tok with her to buy some fat for the moose Maxx had shot only a couple days earlier. She explained to Casey that she was very fussy over what kind of fat they used when they butchered and dressed a moose. It needed to be clean and fresh or she wouldn't mix it with her moose meat.

Because Casey was eager to learn everything about living off the land, she asked Anna if she could use an extra pair of hands to help butcher the moose. She was very agreeable but needed to check with Maxx before she could give the final okay. Casey was not surprised. She knew Maxx thought of her as a greenhorn and, even worse, that she had no business moving to Alaska alone and without a man. He was right about one thing, she did feel like a greenhorn; the word he liked to use was a "cheechako". At the time Casey didn't know what the word meant, but she knew she didn't like it. Maxx was definitely underestimating her and she was looking forward to the opportunity when she would be able to prove herself to the "Big Alaskan sourdough" and gain a little respect. In spite of Maxx, she did welcome the opportunity to drive to Tok with Anna so she could get to know her better. Before they left, she decided to call Robyn to see if she or Jed needed her to pick anything up for them while they were in town. Jed and Jonah were coming over in a couple of days to take down the trees on Casey's property, while she would be helping Robyn clear the garden and can for the winter. Robyn asked Casey to pick up some canning lids for her in town and then suggested that she pick up a few canning jars for herself, since there would be more than enough produce for her and Jed and she was welcome to can whatever they didn't need for the winter. Casey thought how great it would be to have some canned vegetables out of the garden for winter.

It was a cloudy day with a hint of rain in the air when Anna and Casey set out for Tok the next morning. Casey was admiring the view of the Alaska Range foothills covered with a forest of spruce trees and muskegs. There were occasional potholes where moose could often be seen feeding on the moss just below the surface of the water.

Anna looked around. "You can almost always see a moose or two along this stretch of road. It's still hunting season, so they may be in the back country where it's safe, but keep your eye out anyway."

"I will." Casey looked out the window. "The scenery is breathtaking. This is the first time I have been on this part of the Cutoff as a passenger instead of the driver. I can see so much more of the countryside, and the beautiful landscape views are stunning."

Anna agreed, "Yes, I know. I love the Alaska Frontier. This is one of the few places left on this planet where a person can visit or even live out in the wild. Maxx is getting older and has concerns about us living out here in the bush for too much longer. Lately, he has been talking about moving to the lower forty-eight or at least spending winters outside."

Casey had only lived in Slana for a couple of weeks but she understood completely what Anna was talking about. It was a whole different way of life. The rules were different here than they were in the lower forty-eight. People needed each other to just survive. It didn't matter whether people got along with each other or not, you helped your neighbor if he was in need. You shared your meat and what food you might have or your tools if your neighbor needed it whether you wanted to or not. It was the Alaskan way and Casey was catching on fast. She learned that there was a law in Alaska that forbid a motorist to pass by another motorist stranded in his vehicle on the side of the road. Not stopping could easily cost that person his life, especially during the bitter cold winter months, when temperatures could drop to seventy below. It seemed strange to Casey that such a beautiful, serene place could kill someone in just a heartbeat.

As they came to a hairpin curve and started slowing down, they heard an animal wailing in anguish. Over to the right, just ahead was a cow moose with a young calf that had been hit by a passing vehicle. She wasn't more than fifty feet from the side of the road. The young calf lay still as its mother howled in distress. Anna pulled over to the side of the road and reached into the backseat for her rifle. She carefully opened the door on the driver's side, ordering Casey to stay in the truck. She waited as she stood next to the door of her truck. The cow moose looked directly at Anna and continued to cry for her young calf for another couple of minutes. The mother moose seemed to sense that Anna was not there to harm her as she slowly moved a few yards back from her injured calf. Tears came to Casey's eyes as the gunfire rang out and echoed throughout the valley. The sound of the mother's cries gradually diminished and she moved on into the nearby brush.

When Anna came back to the truck and saw Casey wiping her eyes, she said with a caring voice, "You'll get used to it. It's the way it can be out here; it's the way of the land. Come with me, we need to say a prayer over the young moose, to thank him for the gift of his life so you can have meat on your table this winter." Casey followed Anna over to where the moose lay and they both prayed.

Only minutes later Casey had her first lesson in gutting and dressing down a moose. She didn't say much to Anna while they worked alongside each other, cutting the poor animal. At that time Casey would have preferred to buy whatever meat she needed at the grocery store in Tok or Glennallen. She definitely felt like a cheechako and knew she needed to toughen up a bit.

The two of them were able to lift the remains of the young calf and threw him in the back of the truck. They washed up in a nearby pothole just up the road and then continued their trip into Tok.

Anna said, "We need to call the troopers as soon as we get to Tok to let them know how we came about this moose and why we had to shoot him. Someone is sure to see the animal in the back of my truck, and it's illegal to shoot a calf that young."

"That's a good idea. Jed told me that the troopers keep a list of residents that sign up for 'road kill.' When an animal gets hit by a car, the troopers will call the next person on the list to go pick up the animal while the meat is still good."

Anna gave a sign of relief. "Yes it's a good thing that people look after one another out here. Some of the older residents who no longer hunt would sign up for a 'road kill.' That's another good reason why we need to call the troopers. I'm sure it's okay to keep the animal, but it's always good to check."

Thirty minutes later the women pulled into Three Bears Grocery Store, where Anna needed to pick up the pork fat for the moose they were going to process in a couple of days. The butcher was kind enough to put in some extra fat for Casey's moose. While Anna called the troopers to report the moose incident, Casey shopped around and found canning jars and extra lids for Robyn and picked up plenty of the freezer paper that they would need to wrap the meat.

When the women met up at the front of the store, Anna said, "We're in the clear with the troopers—you can keep the moose."

"Great," Casey replied. "Are you about ready to go?"

"Yes, but I have to get my cappuccino. Three Bears just got this fancy machine from the lower forty-eight, and it makes the best coffee you ever tasted. I never come to Tok without having my cappuccino for the drive home."

Casey thought, *I guess no one has ever heard of a Starbuck's or had a latte around here. The things we take for granted.* Casey was beginning to see all the things that were not available in the Alaska bush that you could easily get outside or possibly in Anchorage.

Instead of making a sarcastic remark, she said, "Me too, I want one for the ride home."

The drive home was pleasant while she savored the taste of her cappuccino. She was anxious to get out of her bloody clothes, so Anna dropped her off at her cabin without delay. Casey went straight to the generator shed and started up the generator so she could take a hot shower. She was grateful to have hot running water, something she would have taken for granted before she came to live in the bush.

Chapter Nine: Getting Ready for winter

The next couple of days were leisurely days. Casey straightened up the cabin and worked on building some cabinets in the kitchen area. She was getting used to the generator and learning the best times to run it to maximize her use and save diesel fuel. Casey was beginning to understand what Jonah had been trying to tell her, that you had to keep things as simple as possible; otherwise it could be too expensive to live out in the wilderness. To survive comfortably out here, Casey had to keep things simple. She was hoping that her septic system and water pipes would do all right in the harsh winter to come.

Jonah and Jed were due in about an hour to start clearing the trees around the cabin and river bank. It was going to be a big job, and she was glad Maxx had offered to come down with his front loader to help. They were planning on being done by the end of the day. Casey planned on spending most of the day with Robyn clearing out the garden and canning what produce was left. There was still a lot of work that needed to be done before winter. Maxx had two moose hanging out in his shed to dry, and they were planning on butchering them in a few days. Moose season was just ending and the berry picking was next on the agenda. Casey was beginning to appreciate the Alaskan saying, "There are only two seasons in Alaska: winter and getting ready for winter."

Maxx, Jed, and Jonah all showed up at the same time. They walked around the property, marking the trees that needed to come down and in what order. Their three chain saws started buzzing, which I'm sure could be heard up and down the river for at least a mile or two. Casey briefly thought of the cow moose and her young calf living in the brush on her property. I'm sure she wasn't very happy with all the noise and commotion. Since Casey didn't care for all the noise either, she decided to take her pressure cooker and canning supplies over to Robyn's and get started on clearing the garden and making the salsa and pasta sauce.

Robyn was working out in the garden when Casey arrived. She put her canning supplies in the house and joined her in the garden.

Robyn waved and called out from the other side of the garden, "It's good to see you. Why don't you grab that shovel and start digging up what's left of those potato plants, and I'll pull onions and carrots."

Casey picked up the shovel. "What about the green house? What needs to be picked in there?"

"Jed picked the tomatoes and peppers before he went over to your place this morning. They're in the house ready to be made into salsa and pasta sauce. We still need to pick the cucumbers and green beans."

Casey started digging up the potatoes "As soon as I clean up these rows of potatoes, I can move to the green house for the beans and cukes."

"Sounds like a plan," Robyn said enthusiastically.

The women had worked side by side for only a couple of minutes when they heard tree limbs breaking and hoofs stomping from the nearby woods behind Robyn's house. It was the cow moose and her baby calves, charging out of the brush straight for them. The mama moose was angry and snorting, her hair standing straight up off the top of her huge head. She was in a state of panic as she ran toward them. She was so afraid, she didn't seem to see Casey or Robyn; she just kept coming. Both women froze in their tracks, afraid to run, knowing that the moose would only attack and could outrun them easily. Suddenly, Robyn dropped to the ground, covered her head and put herself in a fetal position. Casey followed suit as the moose and her calves stomped right past them in a dead heat. The moose was within inches of them as she kicked up the garden soil and covered them with dirt.

The moose clomped by, stomping the unpicked produce in the garden, and then quickly made a right turn. They found their way to the other side of the woods and disappeared into the tall brush. Casey screamed and rushed over to Robyn. "Are you all right? Did she get you? Can you move?"

Robyn lay still on the ground for a few seconds, then looked up at Casey and smiled. "That is as close as I ever want to get to a mad mama moose. Those crazy men over at your place with those screaming chain saws scared the hell out of that poor moose and her babies. They're gone now and we're okay, but why don't we go inside and brew some hot tea and use this break time to make the salsa and pasta sauce?" They hugged each other and went inside for that cup of tea.

They spent the next couple of hours preparing and canning the pasta sauce and salsa. Casey looked around the yard for the moose and when she saw that the coast was clear she returned to the garden to finish harvesting the potatoes. After bringing in a couple bushels of potatoes and a few boxes of carrots, she told Robyn that she was headed to the green house to pick the rest of the beans. They decided to leave the cucumbers and onions for another time. They worked all day in the kitchen with two pressure cookers boiling all day. Casey was in awe over all the food they had prepared for the winter months and was looking forward to berry picking and jelly making in a couple of weeks. Living in the bush was going to be hard work, but the feeling of being self-sufficient was very gratifying, and she loved it. After another cup of hot tea and a delicious bowl of Robyn's homemade salmon chowder, they decided to check on the men to see how many trees they had brought down.

Maxx clearing land on Casey's property

Work continues on Casey's cabin

When they arrived at the cabin, they were amazed at the number of trees that they were able to cut down. Maxx was a big help with his front loader moving the trees and clearing the earth around the cabin. Jed had picked out the trees that he wanted for his driveway, and Maxx had moved them to the far side of the property, where he planned on lifting them onto his trailer and would later haul them over to Jed's place. Jonah was busy cutting logs and Jed was splitting the wood, getting it ready for winter. It seemed to Casey that people who lived in the bush were always at work preparing for winter. She wondered what they did in the winter months; hopefully it would be a time of rest and to visit with friends.

Earlier that morning before the men started work, Jed had put several fish lines in the Slana River to catch fish for their dinner. Hopefully there would be plenty for everyone. It was nearly 8 p.m. when Jonah proposed that they call it a night and suggested that they start a bon-fire. There were plenty of tree limbs to burn, and everyone was ready to quit. Jed ran down to the river bank and pulled out the fish—eight burbit and six whitefish. There was plenty of fish to feed everyone. Maxx gave Anna a call and told her to bring the john boat down river to Casey's cabin. Robyn and Casey cleaned the fish and put them on the grill while the men jumped in the river to clean up. It was late, but everyone seemed to have found their second wind.

They all took turns feeding the fire while they passed the platter of fish around for all to eat. It was the best fish Casey had ever tasted; fresh out of the river and right onto the grill. Casey was pleased by the hospitality and friendship she was receiving from her new neighbors.

During the conversation Casey overheard Maxx talking to Jonah about needing to move "Tennessee Luke's" cabin from the lot in back of Midway to a small piece of land Luke had bought about a half-mile down the Cutoff.

Maxx scratched his head and with real concern told Jonah and Jed, "I'm not sure we can safely move that cabin. My trailer is a twenty-foot trailer, and that cabin will hang over the sides. We can jack it up and get it on the trailer and my old five-ton Ford pick-up can pull it slowly down the Cutoff, but maneuvering that beast over that gravel road and through the woods is another story. I'll have to back it up and serpentine through the trees and set it down over Luke's home site with the pipes and septic tank lining up, and to make matters even worse, it slants downhill."

Casey turned toward Jonah. "Who is Tennessee Luke? Does he live in Slana?"

Jonah answered, "No, not yet. He's been living in Glennallen but has been staying in a small cabin that he bought from Katy and Adam. The cabin was a small gift shop that was located next to Midway. The gift shop never amounted to anything, so Katy and Adam sold it to Luke. The cabin is 15'x24', and Maxx promised Luke that he would move it to his home site up the road. Looks like it's turning into a real ugly situation because Maxx doesn't think he can back it onto the pilings of the foundation because it sits on a hill. To make matters even worse, that 1946 old Ford pickup of Maxx's doesn't have very good brakes."

Casey smiled. "Maybe I could look at the cabin and the foundation, and with some measuring we could figure out what it will take to get that cabin in there. You do remember, I'm a truck driver and have been backing fifty-three-foot trailers into tight holes for the past three years. I'm good at 'blind siding' too. Are you familiar with that term?"

"Yes, I'm familiar with that term." Jonah snickered with a little smile on his face. "The question is, do you think you could do it?"

"I might be able to," Casey answered with a sly attitude. "We might have to take out a couple of trees if the measurements don't match up, but you guys are good at that. But what about those bad brakes on that old pickup truck?"

Maxx was listening intently to the conversation between Jonah and Casey and jumped in. "I'll take care of those brakes, no need to worry about that. Can you really back that cabin onto the foundation?"

"It doesn't take brute strength to drive or back up a trailer," Casey said, "just a lot of practice, which I do have. I also have a commercial driver's license, so I can legally pull that cabin and trailer."

Jed hopped into the conversation. "Legal? You've gotta be kidding, none of this is legal. You could never get permits to make this legal, no matter what kind of license you have. Maxx's brakes on that truck are no good. You better be planning to do this in the middle of the night. You don't want the troopers finding out about it."

"Okay, Okay, calm down, we're just going to look into the situation for now," Casey suggested with a reassuring voice. "Let's talk about something else. When do we get to butcher those two moose, Maxx?"

Maxx replied absently, as if his mind was still wondering about the little cabin. "They'll be ready to butcher next week. They're still drying out in the barn."

The mood changed and lighter conversation was welcomed by everyone. Robyn went on to tell about school starting in a couple days and how she was looking forward to the new school year. Robyn had been teaching students at Slana Elementary School for the past three years. Lena Carole, Robyn's supervisor, had an actual teaching credential; Robyn, who had a couple years of college, was able to teach under her supervision. She enjoyed the children and found teaching to be very satisfying. There were twelve children enrolled for the upcoming school year. In rural Alaska, there was a minimal number of students that were required to enroll in order for the state to employ teachers and allow the school to be open for the year. Slana Elementary School had met their quota for students, so Robyn had a job teaching this winter.

Robyn turned to Casey. "Are you interested in teaching school?" There weren't any openings at the Slana Elementary School, but she had heard that the elementary school in the village of Chistochina was looking for a substitute teacher.

Casey was intrigued by the thought of teaching Athabascan children. "I don't have any experience as a teacher, but I have a Master's in Social Work. Do you think they would hire me as a substitute?"

"Yes, I think there is a good chance of it. They have a woman teaching at the school that has a degree in teaching and her assistant lives in Chistochina and is married to an Athabascan native. If you got the job, you would be working under their supervision. The school has two small class rooms and a gym for the kids to play in during the cold winter months. You would be teaching K through 8, but there would always be another teacher there with you."

Robyn and Jed were very reassuring that Casey would make a good teacher while reassuring her that she would have a lot to offer the students due to living "outside" all of her life. Casey agreed but also thought it would be a wonderful opportunity for her to learn the ways of the Ahtna people as well. She agreed to give it some thought in the next couple of days.

Maxx was quiet and gave no opinion as far as Casey and the teaching job. Casey was not even sure he heard the conversation between the rest of the neighbors; he was still mulling over in his mind on how to get Tennessee Luke's cabin up the road and through those trees without a disaster.

Chapter Ten: Butchering the Moose

Casey woke the next morning to the telephone ringing. It was 9 a.m. when she rolled over to answer the phone. She was not accustomed to over-sleeping, but she knew that it was worth a couple of extra hours of sleep to have her land cleared and the brush burned. It was Anna on the other end of the line. Maxx had asked her to let Casey know that they would be butchering the moose in four days. Casey was to be at their home Friday at 7 a.m. because Maxx wanted to get an early start. It was going to take most of the day to cut up, process, and wrap up the moose meat. Maxx also asked Anna if Casey would be willing to take a drive with him to check out Tennessee Luke's cabin and the road he would have to drive over to get the cabin to Luke's home site. The cabin would need to be lowered onto the pilings of the foundation, and he wanted Casey's opinion of the situation. He had already asked Jonah and they were planning on going that afternoon. Casey was happy to join them.

Maxx and Jonah showed up in the old Ford pickup in the early afternoon, and they drove down to Midway to check out the cabin and Maxx's twenty-foot trailer. Both were in good condition, but Maxx's five-ton pickup truck was another story. The brakes were bad, although the truck would be able to pull the cabin and trailer. After they drove to Tennessee Luke's home site, Casey could see why Maxx was so concerned. There were three trees on the property that had to come down. Worse yet, the cabin and trailer would have to be backed in all the way from the Cutoff. Just off the Tok Cutoff was a large gravel pit that they could turn around in, and then they would be able to back the cabin all the way into the home site, where they could directly position it over the pilings of the foundation. Even with the three trees taken out, it was still a very tight squeeze. They did the necessary measuring to be certain that it could even be done. Maxx was still leery and admitted that he didn't think he could back it in. Casey offered to do the driving as well as backing the cabin in as long as there were spotters on all sides of the cabin and trailer.

Casey at her cabin before the land was cleared

Moose out in the bush close to Tennessee Luke's cabin

Maxx getting ready for Tennessee Luke's cabin

Jonah took Casey aside. "Do you think you can really do it? You know you don't have anything to prove to Maxx."

"I know Maxx thinks I'm a 'cheechako,' and he might be right on that account, but I am a very good 'backer' and I really think I can do it, if I just take my time."

So it was settled, Casey would do the driving and Jonah, Maxx, and Jed would be the spotters. The men planned to cut down the three trees in the next couple of days. Tennessee Luke could use the felled trees to line his driveway with, and extra firewood would come in handy this winter. It was easy to see how everything in the bush was always used for one thing or another. Nothing was ever wasted.

For the next couple of days Casey worked around her cabin, continuing to build her kitchen cabinets and doing more cleanup on the property. She hadn't seen the cow moose and her calves since the day they almost ran her and Robyn down in the garden. Casey figured the moose and her calves were long gone, headed into the back country away from people and chain saws.

Casey had mixed feelings about wanting to live in the bush and disturbing the natural habitat of the wild animals that made the Alaska frontier their home. As she went in the house to take a break, she thought, *We just don't live in a perfect world.*

Within the next couple of days Jonah and Maxx had taken out the three trees on Tennessee Luke's property, while Jed and Luke made certain the pipes, the well and septic system were in place. They still needed to check the pilings to make sure the foundation was secure and could hold the cabin. It was going to be a big undertaking, and the few residents living in Slana were talking about coming out for the event. Casey just hoped the troopers didn't get wind of it. She was worried about the brakes on Maxx's truck.

The afternoon passed and after dinner Casey decided to take a walk on the trail down by the river close to her cabin. In the distance she could hear a motor that sounded like a four-wheeler coming down the trail. The noise gradually got louder until she saw an ATV coming toward her, and the driver was a woman with strawberry blonde hair. It was Robyn. She had an application in her hand from the school district for a teacher's position. Casey jumped on the back of Robyn's ATV and they headed for the cabin to sit out on the deck and enjoy a cup of hot tea. Casey had decided that she was going to apply for the substitute position at Chistochina School.

When the school board called her and asked her to come to Glennallen for an interview, she was delighted and felt hopeful that she might get the job. Her interview went well and she became the new substitute teacher for Chistochina Elementary School. Since Casey had no experience as a teacher, they recommended that she shadow the main teacher, Bernie, for three days, allowing her to become familiar with the different grade levels and lesson plans. There were only twelve students enrolled in the school.

Casey's first day shadowing Bernie was fun but very challenging. There were very few students and all in different grades, which meant a lot of preparation for all the lesson plans. Teaching three or four grades at one time meant Casey would need to improve her multi-tasking skills. The good thing about teaching so many grades at once was she would be allowed to come in as early as she wanted on the days that she was to substitute to go over the lesson plans. Casey could understand why the school had two classrooms and two full time teachers. Even though there might only be one child in any particular grade, they all deserved a good education. It was good to learn that the rural children in Alaska were not forgotten, and they took the phrase "No child left behind" very seriously.

All of the children enrolled in the school were Athabascan and were taught to always respect their elders and the traditional ways of their heritage. The children spoke English, but the Ahtna language was taught every day by the two teachers, Bernie and Caroline. Casey knew that this might pose a problem for her since she knew none of the Ahtna language. She learned quickly that it is a very simple language and was given a book to familiarize herself with many of the words.*

Casey commented to Bernie, "The children already know their native language so much better than I could ever teach them. The students are of a whole different culture that I know very little about. Even some of the little ones know how to mush with a dog sled and trap for game with their parents. Things I know nothing about!"

Bernie smiled. "Don't be a worry wart. It's true the kids do know a whole lot of things that you haven't had a chance to learn yet, but think of what you can bring to them. Our planet is getting smaller and smaller due to technology, and 'the old ways' can slip away from the minds of these young children. Let the Elders worry about that and remember that all education is good. Many of the children will leave Chistochina and the Copper River Valley and will move to Anchorage or even outside. They need to learn both ways of life. So, can you now see what you have to offer the children and why it is a good thing that you are here?"

Casey said in a timid voice, "Yes, I can see it. I will do my best to teach them well, but I must admit that I will be learning every bit as much as they are learning."

Bernie grinned. "Wait until you meet one of the elders who comes to teach every Wednesday afternoon. She teaches the children about 'the old ways' and what life was like when she was a young girl and only had sled dogs to rely on for transportation. You definitely will learn more than the students that day. She also teaches traditional beading."

Casey laughed. "Wow, I can't wait. If you have to get sick and stay home, why don't you do it on a Wednesday?"

Bernie smiled. "Or better yet, why don't you just come by on a Wednesday afternoon and sit in on the traditional session? You are always welcome."

"I'll take you up on that."

Casey was so excited about her new job as a teacher, she could hardly wait to get back to Slana and tell everyone her good news. Being a substitute teacher was the perfect part-time job that could even bring in a little extra income. What an opportunity for her. Living out in the Alaska bush was bringing many unexpected blessings.

****

In a couple of short days, Maxx was on the phone telling Casey it was time to butcher the moose. Casey drove to their home, ready to learn a new skill. Anna and Maxx had quartered both moose and carried them down to their basement, where the "butcher shop" was. When Casey followed them to the basement, she was amazed at the setup they used to cut and process the meat. There were three large tables covered with plastic tablecloths. In front of one table was a large band saw that was used to cut through the large, thick bone of the moose. One table had a grinder connected to it and was used to grind moose meat and to mix it with the pork fat that Anna and Casey had bought in Tok. On the second table were sharp butcher knives ready to cut the meat into steaks and roasts. It was quite the set up. The third table was the wrapping and stacking table. Anna and Casey were assigned to that table, which pleased Casey to no end. She was not crazy about the idea of using that band saw on that poor little moose that Anna shot in the head on their drive to Tok.

They heard footsteps upstairs and then Jonah called out, "Anyone home? I heard there's a butchering party going on."

Casey called out, "We're here, downstairs, but I wouldn't say this is any kind of a party." Casey was unsure of how she felt about butchering an animal, especially after seeing them struggle to live and survive in their own natural habitat.

Jonah clattered down the stairs and into the room, saying hello to Maxx. He made his way over to Casey and smiled. "It's something we all had to get used to, especially when we come here from the outside. Young children living in the bush grow up with it and realize it's the way nature is set up. When we live side by side with wild animals and nature is always at our doorstep, we become part of that cycle. That is why we have respect for the animals that we kill and why we pray over them and thank them for their gift to us. So why don't we all stop and pray. Casey, would you like to say the prayer?"

Casey felt a little choked up as she began her prayer. "Lord God, Heavenly Father, we come to you on this day asking you to bless this meat and the animals that gave their lives up so we can have food this winter. Always help us to respect your planet and the gifts of life that you have given us. Help all of us, Lord, to remember that we are part of that cycle of life and not separate from it. May we all live in harmony and love one another."

When Maxx heard Casey's prayer, he walked over to her and gave her a big bear hug. "We all have something to learn from one another, whether we come from outside or have lived in the bush our whole lives." He grinned shyly. "I think this means I'm going to have to stop calling you a 'Cheechako.'"

Everyone roared with laughter! And then it was time to get to work. Maxx and Jonah took to their position at the band saw and began to cut the meat. Casey began to see how the moose was processed and how it turned into a roast or steaks and what would be processed into moose ground round. Anna knew exactly how much pork fat was to be added when they ground the meat. It was amazing how everyone worked in unison. Casey was the primary wrapper, taking each piece of meat and wrapping it tightly in freezer paper and then stacking it in piles at the end of the table. Processing and wrapping up the two moose took seven hours with one short lunch break.

At the end of the day Maxx took one of the large moose steaks and threw it on the grill while Anna and Casey peeled enough potatoes for the four of them. They had the last of the lettuce greens from their garden and made a huge salad. It was more of a feast than a dinner. Casey realized that all of the food that was served came from the land, including the desert, frozen raspberries that Anna picked from last year's batch.

They ended the day with good conversation, sitting around Maxx and Anna's fireplace, enjoying a hot cup of tea. Casey shared her excitement with the group about her new job as a substitute teacher at Chistochina Elementary

School and was given much encouragement. Maxx, the old Alaskan Sourdough, told everyone stories from years ago when he was young and moved to the bush. One of the Ahtna elders took him under his wing and taught him how to run a trap line for game and furs, a skill that he was able to pass on to others, including Jonah.

Soon the conversation turned to Tennessee Luke's cabin and when they would be ready to make the move. Jonah had run into Luke down at Midway yesterday evening and told him that the three trees were removed and the measurements were figured and everyone agreed that Casey was the best one to drive and maneuver the cabin back through the woods and onto his foundation. Tennessee Luke wanted to check his piling and septic system before he gave the final okay to move the cabin. The date was set for two days, weather permitting.

Chapter Eleven: Moving Tennessee Luke's Cabin

Living in Slana was exhilarating for Casey. She was beginning to understand what it meant to be self-sufficient and living off the land, and at the same time what it meant to live in an interdependent community. Moving Tennessee Luke's cabin meant they all had to work together to get the job done. The community was not dependent on the larger society; they depended on each other to figure things out, and the people of Slana lived by their wits. It would be an amazing feat to move that cabin backing it through the woods, but Casey was up to the challenge.

The day had come, Saturday morning, and it appeared that everyone in Slana came out for the big event. About a dozen people were standing around Midway waiting and watching to see how they were going to pull it off. Jed and Robyn had just shown up, and Casey was inside Midway having a cup of coffee with Katy.

Casey looked out the window into the parking lot, where the cabin sat ready to be lifted. She told Katy, "Jed just drove in with Robyn, but we're still waiting for Maxx and Jonah. We were supposed to all meet here at 9:30 to go over the plans before we try and move the cabin. It appears that the townspeople were afraid we would leave early, and they didn't want to miss out on the action."

Katy laughed. "They came to watch you, 'the cheechako,' drive down the road hauling that cabin on Maxx's little trailer. I think they doubt that you all can do this. Tennessee Luke is a little nervous too."

"Well, I can understand that. A lot of things have to fall in place, and there isn't much room for error. Luke has a lot riding on us and our ability to get the cabin moved to his land, and all in one piece." She ignored the cheechako comment.

Just then Jonah and Maxx walked in the door. Jonah looked at Casey and smiled. "Are you ready for all this? Maxx and Jed are ready to start jacking up the cabin, and then we'll slide the wooden planks one by one under the cabin on each side until we get it high enough to back Maxx's trailer underneath. Do you want to watch?"

Casey laughed. "Of course, but let's make sure we're all on the same page once we leave Midway and head down the Cutoff."

It took over an hour to slowly jack up the cabin, an inch at a time, until there were enough 16" x 20" timbers in place holding up the structure. It took more manpower than Maxx and Jonah figured, but there were plenty of sightseers to help out. Slana was an amazing little settlement where everyone was ready to do whatever they could to get the job done. Katy kept the coffee flowing and offered it to all the sightseers. Even a few natives from Chistochina came down to watch the show. Casey was hoping that the state troopers had not gotten wind of what they were all up too. They had no permits to move that cabin. The only saving grace was that the cabin was so heavy, they could only move about 10 miles an hour down the road.

It was time. They had the cabin level, and Casey got in Maxx's truck and backed the trailer right under the cabin without any trouble. They then removed the jacks and wooden planks and the cabin rested on top of Maxx's twenty-foot flatbed trailer. Jonah put red flags on the back corners of the cabin. Everyone cheered and Tennessee Luke was a little less anxious. They were on their way; Maxx drove his SUV a good hundred yards out in front of the moving cabin, warning any drivers coming in the opposite direction that a wide load was coming up behind him. Jed and Jonah drove their four-wheelers alongside the cabin as Casey drove down the road. Tennessee Luke was trailing behind the cabin on his four-wheeler. Maxx's 1946, five-ton Ford pickup was able to pull the cabin, but it was slow going. So far Casey didn't need to use the brakes because the load was so heavy, but she still had concerns about being able to stop if they needed to go down a hill. It would have been better to use a newer truck to pull the cabin, but no one had a truck with as much horse power as Maxx's old Ford pick-up. It was just going to have to do.

The turnoff to Luke's property was about a half-mile down the road. The road from Midway to the turnoff to Luke's property was flat and well paved, so the truck brakes, at this point, were not an issue. It took a good thirty minutes to get to the old gravel pit where Tennessee Luke's turnoff to his property was located. From here on into Luke's home site was either a dirt or gravel road. When Casey came to the turnoff, she had to back it in from the Tok Cutoff. Once she turned off the main road, it would be backing in over a quarter of a mile all the way to the home site. At this point Maxx left his SUV at the gravel pit and Jed and Jonah parked their ATVs. The residents from Slana followed them into the gravel pit and left their vehicles parked. Maxx, Jed, and Tennessee Luke were the three spotters who gave Casey direction as she tried to back up while maneuvering the cabin through the trees.

Jonah jumped in the passenger's side of the old Ford pickup. "I'm here for moral support, and an extra pair of eyes might help too. Just take it slow."

Casey chuckled. "I can't take it any other way." Casey slowly backed down the gravel road toward Tennessee Luke's home site. The road was narrow, not leaving any room on either side. Willows and brush covered Jed, Maxx and Luke up to their waists as they tried to keep Casey in eyesight of the rear view mirrors on the old truck. Jonah was nervous and at that point not much help. Casey knew how to back up a fifty-three-foot trailer into very tight spots, and this was no different; she just had to go slow, which was not a problem for her. After a couple hundred feet of backing the cabin straight back on the old gravel road, Casey saw the trees that she had to serpentine through to get the cabin to the home site. This is where the challenge would begin. Jonah was jumpy and anxious, so Casey told him that she needed a spotter out in front of the truck, someone she could always see and hear. The old truck was loud and she had to back through very tight spots without seeing where she was going through the trees. Jonah would be in a much better position to communicate with the other spotters, which in turn would help Casey when she could not see the edges of the cabin. It took real team work; inch by inch they were getting the job done and maneuvering through the trees.

As they came closer to the actual home site, Casey could see Maxx's Caterpillar sitting over to the side of the log foundation where she was to put the cabin down. The septic system and pipes for the cabin were built in the ground and were ready to be hooked up once the cabin was in place. The problem Casey saw was that the foundation was built into the hillside. The cabin had to be placed on the foundation from a downhill slant. That meant Casey would have to back down the hill's slight decline to the cabin. She told Jonah that the brakes on the old five-ton pickup wouldn't hold, and the whole mess, including her, would go tumbling down the hillside. Jonah called a time out. It was past lunch time and everyone was hungry anyway.

Anna pulled out several pint jars of smoked salmon that she had canned during salmon season only a couple of months ago. She brought enough to feed everyone, and Robyn brought two boxes of saltines. They had a salmon feast right there in the middle of the woods while they discussed what needed to be done to get the cabin on top of the foundation. Giving up was not an option. They all agreed that the brakes on Maxx's truck could not hold the cabin if Casey tried to back it up and set the cabin down on a foundation that was built on the slope.

Maxx came up with a solution. "Why not hook up my cat with a chain onto the front of the truck while Casey backs the cabin over the foundation. The caterpillar can be the brakes that the truck doesn't have. I'll be on the cat holding everything in place, which will give you men a chance to get under the cabin to jack it up and level it out by removing the logs. You'll have to remove one log at a time and lower it down slowly."

Jonah wiped the sweat off his forehead. "Are you sure your caterpillar can hold it long enough for Casey to get the cabin in place and for us to level it out? It sounds too risky to me. We could lose everything, your truck, the trailer, the cabin, the caterpillar—even our lives."

Maxx said in his gruff voice, "Hold on Jonah, nobody's going to get hurt. If the cat starts to slip and it can't hold the truck and cabin, we all jump clear and everything else slides down the hill. I am almost certain my cat can hold it all. I'm willing to risk it. What about you, Luke? You could lose your cabin. Do you want to risk it?"

Luke scratched his head. "I'm willing to risk my cabin, but I don't want anyone getting hurt."

"Nobody's getting hurt," Maxx said in a reassuring voice. "Let's ask some of those sightseers if they want to volunteer to help pull logs out and level out the cabin when we jack it up onto the foundation. We could use a couple more spotters too. We want a man on every corner. The more men we have, the faster we can get this done. What do you think, Casey? Are you up for this?"

Casey smiled. "Count me in, but know if that cat can't hold us, I won't hesitate to jump out before it all goes down the hill."

Jonah told Casey, "You better jump clear, and don't wait until the last minute; it might be too late."

Casey thought to herself, *There he goes again, telling me what to do. He must think I'm an idiot*, but she was not about to get into it with him. She knew tensions were running high, and this was not the time or place. She knew she could do it and she also believed that Maxx and his caterpillar could hold it all.

Jed asked some of the men to help with removing the logs and a couple of women to be spotters. Everyone was ready. Maxx and Jonah fastened the chain to the caterpillar and the truck and Casey started to back the trailer and cabin down the slight decline toward the foundation. Casey had poor visibility due to the size of the cabin but was able to see the top of the log foundation and where the cabin was to rest. The pipes and septic system were lined up as Casey gradually maneuvered the trailer backward, listening to Jonah for instruction on which way to turn. Casey had one eye in the rear view mirror, watching the cabin, and the other eye on Maxx, making sure the caterpillar wasn't slipping. So far their plan was working great. After thirty minutes, which felt like three hours, the cabin was finally maneuvered directly over the logged foundation. Maxx and his cat had to hold onto the truck while Jed, Luke and four volunteers jacked up each corner of the cabin, removing one timber at a time, leveling the cabin out. It was a slow process and Jonah never left Casey's side, keeping her informed to how the work was coming. Basically, her job was finished, but she knew she needed to pay attention and stay alert until the men were finished and she could pull the empty trailer out. Jonah checked with Maxx several times while the men continued to level out the cabin, and just as Maxx said, the caterpillar didn't move an inch.

After three tedious hours, they finally had the cabin level and it sat directly over the foundation. The final word was given and Jonah told Casey to pull the trailer out. When Casey was on level ground again, she was finally able to get out of that old Ford truck and stretch her stiff legs while Maxx took the chain off the truck.

Maxx walked over to her, reached down and gave Casey a big bear hug. He said, "I could have never done what you did and I will never call you a cheechako again; you have my word on that."

Casey laughed.

"I'll hold you to that, and I want you to know that I could have never backed that cabin onto that foundation without your help."

Jonah walked over to Casey and gave her a warm hug, something he had never done before. "You're a real bush woman, not a wanna be." Jonah's statement meant a lot to Casey. She had taken a big step in gaining the respect from everyone in Slana.

Tennessee Luke was going around shaking everyone's hand and thanking them for all their help. It was a true community effort that got Tennessee Luke's cabin on that foundation.

Chapter Twelve: Blueberry Picking with Jonah

Fall in Alaska was an unexpected surprise to Casey. There was a crisp bite to the air, and the golden leaves of the birch trees turned a bright yellow and glimmered in the cool morning breeze. Their colors were striking next to the dark green spruce that covered the foothills of the Alaska Range. Fireweed and thick patches of moss were plentiful amongst the fall foliage. Casey knew winter was right around the corner and she could almost feel snow in the air. Her cabin was winterized with extra insulation around all the pipes that were not buried deep within the soil. Thick sheets of plastic were tacked over the windows to help keep the harsh wind out. She was ready for the harsh winter months ahead when temperatures would drop to 70 below.

While Casey was putting the breakfast dishes in the kitchen sink, she decided to have another cup of coffee out on the deck. One of her favorite things to do early in the morning was to watch the little river otter swim along the bank in search of his breakfast. As she was watching the otter and enjoying her coffee, the telephone rang. It was Bernie from Chistochina School asking Casey if she could sub for her for the following three days. Casey was excited for the opportunity to teach and told Bernie she would be happy to. Bernie told Casey that Caroline would be there all three days while she was subbing and would meet her at 6:30 tomorrow morning to go over the lesson plans with her.

Casey returned to the deck to watch the wild life on the river, and after a while Jonah called and said, "It's a great morning for berry picking. Do you wanna go? I know where there's some good berry patches out past Four Mile." Four Mile Road was four miles out Nebesna Road from the Tok Cutoff. Jonah lived further out Four Mile Road, deeper into the bush, and his place was accessible only by ATV. Casey had never been to Jonah's place, but she knew he lived in a 9'x12' cabin with no running water. The creek ran a quarter of a mile from his cabin, where he hauled his own water every day.

"Yes, I would love some fresh blueberries," Casey said. "I can meet you at the corner of Four Mile and Nebesna Road in an hour. Will that work for you?"

"You bet. I'll bring the berry pickers," Jonah said. Casey wondered what a berry picker looked like; she knew she was about to find out.

It was a brisk, cool fall morning, Foliage was turning shades of orange and rusty brown. Casey left her truck at a nearby gravel pit and got on the back of Jonah's four-wheeler. They were headed several miles back into the deep bush where the berry patches were plentiful and not picked over by other Slana residents or bears.

They came to a stream and Jonah parked his ATV. "My place is only a mile from here back through these woods. The blueberries patches are scattered all through here. They are low bush berries, so they are along the ground and easy to pick with these berry pickers."

Jonah's cabin

The berry picker was a bright red metal scooper with fork like prongs that scooped up the berries when you ran it through the berry patch. Then you had a pail attached to a rope that you hung around your neck. When a person scooped up enough berries they threw them into the pail and moved on to the next patch of berries.

Jonah said to Casey, "We need to always keep each other in our sight or call out to each other frequently. Noise is a good thing out here. Always listen for the sound of the stream so you don't wander off too far. All the willows and brush look the same out here. You can be ten feet away from the road or the water and not see it; plus our heads are looking down where the berry patches are."

Jonah picking blueberries

Casey was learning quickly the do's and don'ts of living in the bush. It was so important to be aware of one's surroundings at all times. Jonah had lived in the bush for several years and she felt safe when he was around.

"Not to alarm you," Jonah added, "but the bears eat these berries too.

They will be going into hibernation soon and are fattening up this time of year. Making plenty of noise lets any bears hanging around know that these berries belong to us. I brought my firearm with me just in case they might have a problem with that."

Casey knew Jonah was serious but was making light of the situation. "What about moose? I see plenty of willows around here, and I know that's their favorite food."

"Yes, they like these woods too, but don't give it any more thought," he said. "We got berries to pick."

Casey and Jonah talked loudly back and forth as they picked bucket after bucket of beautiful, plump blueberries. They talked and laughed about Tennessee Luke's cabin and the ordeal they went through getting it set up. Casey also shared with Jonah that tomorrow was her first day as a substitute teacher at Chistochina School, and she was very excited to be teaching Athabascan students.

When Casey looked up she saw a small cabin peering out through the woods. She was amazed at how far they had traveled while picking berries along the mushy moss floor of the woods amongst the willows and spruce trees. It was Jonah's cabin, and the creek he carried water from was right next to them.

Suddenly, they heard a thundering noise of hooves stomping through the forest and the creek bed. Jonah grabbed a couple of berry buckets and yelled to Casey, "Grab those two berry pails and follow me. It's a herd of Caribou headed right for us." When the animals heard Jonah's voice, they slowed down but kept coming. They made it to the cabin as the caribou stomped through the woods, stopping to graze around Jonah's cabin.

Jonah started laughing. "I didn't really plan this, Casey. This is not the way I wanted to show you my cabin." They both started laughing, but it was a bit awkward.

Casey looked out the cabin window and watched the caribou graze around Jonah's cabin. They were so close she could almost reach out the window and touch them. She wanted to stand on his front porch to get closer to them, but she knew that would be too invasive and she didn't want to intrude on their space. Casey was learning how to co-exist with nature and its wildlife. After a few minutes of watching the caribou, Casey noticed Jonah putting on some hot water for tea. She also noticed that Jonah's tea was made from plants and herbs that he probably gathered from the woods.

Jonah handed her a steaming cup of his homemade tea. "This is my secret brew from the woods. I hope you like it. We probably need to stay here for an hour or so until we're sure that the caribou have moved out. Then we can make our way back to my ATV. What do you think of the tea?"

Casey smiled. "I'm in no hurry to leave, and this tea is delicious."

"It's a blend that the Ahtna people have been using for generations. I'll make up a bag for you before we leave." They drank their tea and continued to watch the caribou. Soon they were beginning to move away from the cabin and started malingering through the brush.

Jonah's cabin was very small, but very tidy and efficient. In the center of the cabin was a potbelly stove that he used to heat the cabin and boil water when needed. Four oil lamps were permanently fixed to the inside logs of his cabin. There was a small two burner propane stove and oven that he cooked on if he didn't want to warm something up on the wood stove. Next to his propane stove was a hand-built wooden cabinet with a tile countertop. His food and supplies, along with a few pots and pans and dishes, were kept in the cabinet. He had a large dish pan that sat on the countertop for doing dishes and cleaning up. His bedroom consisted of a bed, a trunk, and a few wooden pegs nailed to the wall where he hung his clothes and boots. In the center of the room by the wood stove was a beautiful bear rug where two comfortable lounge chairs sat, along with a table and oil lamp for reading. Books and magazines were kept on book shelves that he had made. On one of the window ledges sat a modern telephone, a radio, and a very small TV set that ran off a small generator. Other than a small kitchen table and two chairs, that was all there was in Jonah's cabin. It was a very cozy home and all anyone needed.

When Casey asked him where the bathroom was, he laughed. "No way! No way would I put piping in ten foot underground and then have to insulate the pipes and then watch it freeze during the winter months. Anyway, I have too much permafrost on this property for plumbing. Look through that window and you can see my outhouse. Works just fine, plus I have a honey bucket that I keep under the bed. I even have a makeshift shower outside in those trees that works great during the summer and spring, and the creek is only a quarter of a mile down that path; comes in handy. In the dead of winter I can always take a shower at Midway or Slana School. They have washers and dryers too." Casey had to admit, it was a nice set up.

After giving it a little thought she asked, "Do you think my pipes are going to freeze up this winter?"

Jonah smiled. "I hope not. We did everything we could do. This land out here in the wild with temperatures reaching down to 70 below is just not made for such amenities. I'm not too worried about the pipes and septic; they're buried deep and should be okay. The only pipe we really have to worry about is any pipe that gets exposed to the bitter-cold temperatures or ice-cold wind blowing down through the valley. We may have to do repair work this winter, but for the most part everything is going to work."

Casey was looking forward to the winter months ahead, but she also knew that the cold weather could bring challenges along with the hours of darkness. Casey and Jonah continued to visit with each other for the next thirty minutes when they realized that the caribou were long gone. Casey suggested that they head back through the woods to find Jonah's four-wheeler. It was time for her to get back home and freeze her berries, and she wanted to make a quick stop at Robyn's cabin on her way home. Casey collected the pails of berries while Jonah made up a sack of his secret brew tea for Casey. The four-wheeler was where they had left it, and they were soon traveling down the dirt road, enjoying the rest of a beautiful fall day. When Jonah dropped Casey at her truck, she thanked him for the wonderful day of berry picking and commented how much she enjoyed his company and seeing his cabin. Jonah was also pleased with the day he spent with Casey. As she started to drive away he waved and wished her luck for tomorrow when she was spending the day substituting at Chistochina School. She waved good-bye and said she would let him know how it went.

Driving down Nebesna Road, Casey remembered to make a right turn into Jed and Robyn's place. She wanted to share some of her blueberries with Robyn. She knew this was the end of the season for blueberry picking, and Robyn had talked about making up some jam for the winter. Casey also thought Robyn might have some thoughts about her first day at Chistochina School.

As Casey pulled into the driveway, Jed came to the door and said, "Come on in, Robyn has been trying to reach you by telephone; you've been gone all day. She heard you were subbing for Bernie at Chistochina tomorrow."

Casey answered with a chuckle, "Yes I am. Word sure gets around fast. Sorry I missed your phone call; I've been out berry picking with Jonah. We got the last of the blueberries—the night frost is about to get the rest of them. You won't believe it, but we ran into a small herd of caribou a quarter of a mile from Jonah's cabin. We had to make a run for it and got to his place just in time."

Jed laughed. "Oh yeah, just in time for what? Sounds pretty convenient for Jonah."

Robyn chided Jed. "Stop teasing her. Just ignore him, Casey; he's just stirring up gossip."

Jed laughed out loud. "It's as plain as the noses on your faces. Jonah has a crush on Casey. He never asked me to go berry picking. I bet he doesn't even like blueberries." Jed was now roaring with laughter. "But I can't figure out how he set up the caribou herd." Jed walked out of the room chuckling.

Robyn was clearly annoyed. "Just ignore him, Casey, though I do think he might have a point." She smiled. "Nobody has ever seen the softer side of Jonah till you came to town."

Both women giggled and then Casey changed the subject, "I brought you some blueberries—you said you wanted to make some jam. What's your afternoon look like?"

"Looks good," Robyn answered. "We'll be done in a couple of hours, and that gives us plenty of time to talk about teaching the kids at Chistochina School." Robyn brought out her cooking pot she used for boiling berries and Casey started sifting through the berries, picking out the best ones. Robyn used her Spiced Blueberry Jam recipe that was handed down from her mother. It had won a blue ribbon at the state fair, and even Katy sold it at Midway to the tourist passing through on their way to Anchorage. Robyn and Casey had enough berries for two dozen half-pint jars; enough for Jed and Robyn and Casey, and a few jars were put aside for Jonah.

Jed walked into the kitchen with a concerned look on his face just as Casey and Robyn were finishing up with their spiced blueberry jam. He told the women Maxx had just called to let him know a couple of grizzlies had been seen wandering around and to stay alert. There had been recent forest fires in Alaska due to the unusually hot summer, and the bears were showing up in places they had never been seen before, but at least they weren't causing any problems.

Residents in Slana always kept each other informed with any news and watched out for each other. Jed planned to call Jonah to let him know about the bears, and in turn, Jonah would spread the word further out Four Mile to warn the others of the bear sightings. Jedd told Casey not to worry, that bears usually didn't like getting too close to the Cutoff and where there were more people. Casey was getting used to living out in the bush and wasn't too concerned about the bear warning, but of course she would stay alert.

Caribou crossing the road

Spiced Blueberry Jam

By
Maraley McMichael

5 cups crushed fresh or frozen blueberries

1 cup water

2 Tbsp. lemon juice

½ tsp. ground cinnamon

½ tsp. ground cloves

½ tsp. butter

3 cups sugar

1 package fruit jell (no sugar needed) pectin

7 ½ pint jelly jars with lids

Wash jars and lids with bands. Place jars upright in 9"x13" glass dish ready to fill with boiling water. Place lids and bands in saucepan. Cover with hot water and keep hot over low heat. Fill tea kettle and bring to a boil. Prepare and measure fruit into 6-8 quart saucepot. Add water, lemon juice, spices and butter. Measure sugar and set aside. Gradually stir Fruit Jell pectin into prepared fruit using wire whisk. Do not add all at once. Bring to a boil over high heat, stirring constantly. Just before jam boils, turn off heat long enough to pour boiling water over jars. Stir sugar into boiling fruit mixture. Return to a boil. Boil hard 1 minute, stirring constantly. Remove from heat. Skim foam if necessary. (The butter reduces foam) Empty water from jars and turn upside down on sterile towel for 30 seconds to drain. Upright jars and carefully ladle or pour jam into jars, leaving ¼ inch headspace. Wipe jar edges clean with wet sterile cloth. Place metal lids on jars and screw on bands. Process jars 10 minutes in a boiling water bath canner. Remove jars. Let cool. Check lids for seal by pressing down on the center of the lid. If the lid springs up, it has not sealed, and the jam should be refrigerated.

Chapter Thirteen: Bears in the School Yard

Morning came soon enough for Casey when her alarm went off at 5 a.m. It was time to get up and get ready for school. She ate her oatmeal sprinkled with fresh blueberries, and Robyn's spiced blueberry jam was delicious on her homemade whole wheat toast. By 6 a.m. she was headed for her truck with a thermos of coffee and a backpack full of school supplies that she thought she might need for teaching. Chistochina School was a thirty-minute drive on the Tok Cutoff toward the town of Glennallen. Casey wondered what driving the two-lane road would be like during the winter months when the sky was pitch black and the road was snow packed. She had already been informed that Alaska schools don't get snow days, and the only school days off during the winter is when temperatures reach fifty below or colder. If there was a blizzard, too bad; the kids stood out in the cold until the school bus picked them up. Casey was grateful that she had a one-ton, four-wheel-drive truck with dooly tires in the back. She could drive most anywhere as long as she could see the road.

Casey arrived at the school as Caroline was just pulling up. Caroline handed Casey her own key to the school, knowing that in the future Casey would be coming early to go over lesson plans when she was subbing on her own. Right now she would be shadowing Caroline more than she would be teaching on her own.

Once Casey went inside the school, she could see that there was a large gymnasium with a room of showers and bathrooms attached. The gym was perfect for the kids to get plenty of exercise during the winter months when they were not able to play outside.

Caroline, an attractive woman in her mid-thirties with jet black hair and wide brown eyes, commented, "The people from Chistochina also use the gym for other activities during the winter months, such as dog sled races. The mushers often spend the night in the gym during the races. They also use it for other village activities as well."

Casey was impressed with Chistochina School and all the services it had to offer the children. The state of Alaska seemed to take care of their residents, whether they were living in a town or in a remote village without regular electricity. Casey asked about the electrical power and Caroline told her about the large generator that powered the school. They even had a small room off one of the classrooms that had computers for the students to learn on. Casey could understand why one of the elders came every Wednesday to teach the children of "the old ways"; with computers and knowledge of the modern world, their heritage could be too easily forgotten.

Casey and Caroline went over the lesson plans for all the grades. The plan was for Casey to teach the younger students, kindergarten through third grades, while Caroline was in the other classroom teaching fourth through eighth. After lunch Casey would be teaching a history class to the older students while the younger students would be coloring and drawing. The children showed up for class at eight-thirty and school began with everyone saying the Pledge of Allegiance. Caroline introduced Casey to all twelve students, and they were given thirty minutes to introduce themselves and learn a little about each other. They had a lot of questions about where Casey used to live before she moved to Alaska. The children asked a lot of questions about living "outside" and how it was different from Chistochina. Casey answered questions the best she could and told the children they would have a lot of time to get to know each other as the school year progressed. Ninety percent of the children were native Athabascan; the other ten percent were Caucasian with an Athabascan parent. All of the children lived in the village of Chistochina.

Along with everyday lessons, which included reading, spelling, math, and writing, the children were taught practical ways of living in the bush. They grew up learning from their parents and elders in the village about subsistence living, hunting, trapping, fishing, and dip netting. They were all familiar with canning and smoking salmon. Many of the children hunted moose and caribou with their parents and older siblings. A few of the children were learning dog mushing and some had participated in dog sled races.

Casey knew she had a lot to offer the students as far as lessons in reading and writing and living in the lower forty-eight, but she was very aware of how much she could learn from her students. She only hoped that she would get a lot of opportunity to substitute for Bernie and Caroline.

Class began and the children were much more familiar with the routine of working on their lessons individually and with the help of the teacher. As Casey moved among the students and their different grade levels, it turned out to be easier as she became more skilled at multi-tasking.

Morning went by very quickly and it was time for lunch. All the children and teachers brought their lunch and ate in one classroom. It was a special time when the students got to be together to share the events of the day. Chistochina School had no cafeteria, which was practical due to the few students that attended the school.

During lunch Casey had the opportunity to get to know the children on a more personal level. Several children walked to school or rode their four-wheelers. Younger children were taken to and from school by a parent or relative; most of the students were related to each other or had very close relationships with one another. Everyone knew everybody in Chistochina; like Slana, it was an interdependent settlement.

After lunch the children got to choose whether they wanted to have their recess outside where there was a couple of swing sets and a slide, or in the gym. Today they chose to play outside, due to the nice weather. Winter was right around the corner, and the nice fall days would be few and far between.

After lunch Caroline read to the whole class a story from one of the books in the school library. It was always an ongoing story that was continued each day, and the children looked forward to their story time with each other and the teacher. It also helped to quiet their minds and settle them back into the school routine.

During the afternoon Caroline would be teaching the Ahtna language class where the children became more familiar with their native language. Casey learned that words in the Ahtna language were simple words that had to do with practical applications to the lifestyle of the Athabascan people years ago. The words that were being taught to the children were the words for trees and plants, animals, bugs, fish, ducks, birds, berries and several words that had to do with the earth and the environment.*

After the language class was over Caroline turned to Casey and said, "Technology is being introduced to all rural areas in Alaska, and it is a good thing for the children to learn about the world outside of where they live, but it is equally important for them to not forget their native language and heritage."

Casey agreed completely with her. "Tomorrow is Wednesday; will one of the elders from the village be coming to teach the children of the 'old ways' and traditions?"

Caroline smiled. "Yes, she'll be here in the morning. You're always welcome to sit in on those classes, whether you are subbing or not. The more you learn about the Athna culture, the better it is for the children." Casey agreed and started getting ready for the history class she was about to teach.

Teaching the older students was interesting and challenging with their many questions about whatever they were learning. Soon the school day had ended and the children either left with a family member who was picking them up or walked home on their own. Tired after her first day of teaching school, Casey drove home, looking forward to tomorrow, when a village elder would be visiting the school to teach the children about the "old ways and traditions."

The next day, Casey arrived at the school and let herself in, briefly looking over the lesson plans for the day. Promptly at eight-thirty, the children started filing in, all of them giving Casey a friendly greeting. The routine was the same as yesterday, but today Casey had the lesson plans down and was much more efficient with multi-tasking, helping the students with their different assignments. After a couple of hours, the village elder arrived wearing a handmade parka decorated with shells and seed beads. She smiled and greeted the children with warmth and laughter. It was obvious that all of the children knew and respected the elderly woman. A few children cried out "grandma" and ran to her, arms spread ready for a big bear hug. Within minutes they all gathered around one large table and were silent and ready to hear what the elderly woman had to say. She had brought her needlework, and Casey watched the children bring out their own pieces of needlework that they were working on. The students were of all ages, boys and girls, using tiny seed beads to make their own designs on pieces of leather. While they were sewing their bead work, she spoke to the children about what her life was like when she was a young girl. The only way she traveled during the winter months was by dog sled, when they might travel to Mentasta, another Ahtna Village just north of Slana. She spoke of the time she saw her first white man; she was only sixteen years old. She was a fascinating woman with much knowledge of the old ways.

She clearly loved her heritage, and the children loved and respected her. They all spoke words together from the Ahtna language, and the older woman answered questions the children and Casey had to ask. It was an ideal morning full of storytelling and valuable learning. The elderly woman was soon giving the children hugs and saying her good-byes until next week.

It was lunchtime, Casey's favorite time of the school day because of the personal time she got to spend with the children. Kelly, a kindergartener with olive skin and coal black hair gave Casey a wide, friendly smile as she told her about her dream to win the Iditarod when she grew up and was old enough to race. Her father was a musher and had been in several dog races. Kelly had a small sled that her father had made her, and she was allowed to run with only one dog. Kelly told Casey that when she turned eight years old, her father promised her she could run with two dogs, and as she grew bigger he would allow her to run with more dogs. Casey was so impressed with Kelly and the other student's willingness to learn and try new things.

Caroline called a time out from the chatter. "Well it's time for recess. Who wants to play inside in the gym, and who wants to go outside to enjoy another nice fall day?" The kids all voted to go outside for their recess.

One by one the twelve students followed each other outside, making sure not to forget their soccer ball. Kelly and her friend Maria were playing hide and seek amongst the trees while the older children were picking sides for a game of soccer. The children were yelling and playing on the swing sets and burning off energy from their noon meal.

Suddenly Kelly came running over to Casey screaming in a panic, "There's a big bear over behind that tree and he's looking at me." She began to cry hysterically, frightening the other children. When Casey looked in the direction Kelly had run from, she saw two large, brown bears that she thought were probably grizzlies. They were in the school yard. The older boys heard the screams and went immediately to the younger students and told them sternly to be still, to stop screaming and to follow them quietly into the gym. Casey and Caroline rounded up the children that were playing on the swing set as the bears moved closer.

Grizzlies near Chistochina school

Caroline told Casey in a very calm voice, "Don't make eye contact, get the kids, and slowly move toward the gym." Casey did as she was told with a lump in her throat. One of the older boys was waiting quietly at the door for the two teachers and the remaining students while the rest of the children were kept quiet in the gym. The two grizzlies were about fifty feet away when the boy closed the doors behind the two teachers and the remaining children. They went straight to the gym, where there were no windows, and waited about thirty minutes. Casey told the children about her adventures driving an eighteen-wheeler when she lived outside, while Caroline slipped out of the gym to telephone for help.

Class went on as usual when they returned to the classroom. The younger children were with Casey doing a reading assignment, while Caroline had the older students doing math assignments. While the children did their lessons, Casey glanced outside the school window and saw two men in the woods carrying rifles. One of them was Jonah. She was relieved to know that Caroline had gotten an alert out that there were bears in the school yard. During the student's snack time, parents were notified by Caroline to pick their children up after school or to make other arrangements; no child would be allowed to walk home. A couple of the parents were working in Glennallen, so Casey offered to take home any child who didn't have a safe way home.

The bell rang and school was out. Parents and relatives arrived to take the children home and thanked the two teachers for handling a potentially dangerous situation. No one knew for sure why the two grizzlies showed up that day, but everyone agreed that the bear threat could not be ignored.

After the parents had left with the children, Jonah came out of the woods and said with a chuckle, "Trouble just seems to follow you; a couple of days ago the caribou were after you, and today it was grizzly bears." Jonah was trying to make light of the situation, but Casey wasn't buying it.

Tears welled up in her eyes as she threw her arms around Jonah. "I was so afraid! I wanted to run, but I knew I couldn't. It's dangerous living out here with all these wild animals! How do people do it?"

Jonah held Casey in his arms and let her cry for a few minutes, then gently said, "You're safe now; bears can be very scary, especially when you don't know what they're going to do. You and Caroline kept your wits about you and helped the little ones, and from what I heard the older students really came through. We can all be proud of them."

Casey remembered how the seventh- and eighth-graders reacted and how they knew exactly what to do. She told Jonah, "I'm so proud of them; the outcome could have been very different if they had panicked. But I still think this is a very dangerous place to live."

"Casey, it can be dangerous living anywhere. It's all about knowing the environment you live in, whether you're living in a big city where gangs and shootings happen, or having to fight your way through rush-hour traffic. Isn't it safer here, or at least just as safe as life in the big city, where dangers do exist, only in a different form." Casey had to laugh; she never thought about it in that way before.

As Jonah walked Casey to her car, he said, "You know we have to track those bears down. It's unfortunate that we've had all these fires this summer. The bears are out of their natural habitat, and they might be looking to fatten up before they go into hibernation. We can't have them hanging around the school like this. The bears may have just been curious, we'll never really know, but we can't take those kinds of chances with the children." Casey smiled and said she understood, and Jonah told her he would call her later tonight after he got home.

Chapter Fourteen: Denali Earthquake Rocks the Tok Cutoff

Winter had arrived, and snow covered every inch of the vast frontier. To Casey it looked like a winter wonderland out of the storybooks her mother had read to her as a child. Alaska was the most serene, beautiful place in the world, and Casey loved to walk through the woods in the fresh fallen snow. Dawn would come around 10 a.m.; no sunlight, only twilight that sparkled against the fallen snow. By 4 p.m. the magical twilight was gone and darkness fell upon the land again until the next day. Casey loved winter and didn't miss the sunlight a bit. Outside chores, going to the post office, visiting neighbors, including any shopping that needed to be done in Tok or Glennallen, was done during daytime hours. So far Casey's plumbing in the cabin had not presented any problems. Jonah and Billy Joe had done a good job. Of course, there weren't any blizzards or high winds yet, and the temperatures were holding around ten degrees; beautiful winter weather.

All that disappeared on November 3, 2002 around 12:30 p.m. when the ground began to rumble. At first it was obvious to Casey that it was an earthquake; she had experienced them before in California when she was driving her eighteen-wheeler. Within a few seconds it grew to a horrific, violent jolt that knocked her to the floor of the cabin. She tried to get up, but the force of the jolt knocked her down again. She tried to crawl to the center of the cabin where she wouldn't get hit by falling debris. Her grandmother's cabinet came crashing down to the floor, and shattered glass sprayed everywhere. The propane refrigerator, connected by a metal pipe to the huge propane tank outside, was pulsating across the room when the refrigerator door flew open, throwing out last night's lentil soup all over the floor. She looked up and saw the walls and roof of her cabin shifting violently back and forth. She felt sure it was coming down on top of her, and there was nothing she could do to save herself. She could hear herself screaming, but it felt like it wasn't really her. In another moment she was on the ceiling looking down at a screaming Casey trying to crawl to safety with flying glass and debris falling all over her and the cabin.

Then it was over; complete silence. The cabin was still standing, but the floor didn't feel solid. It felt like it was wiggling, like a bowl of jelly. At least she

99

could stand up as she tried to make her way toward the propane stove and refrigerator to make sure nothing was severed. She passed by the kitchen window and saw a red pickup truck racing down the Cutoff at full speed, screeching tires, barely missing her driveway as it pulled in, taking out a couple of small birch trees as it bolted down the drive toward her cabin. It was Jonah, slamming on his brakes, jumping free of his truck, and running toward the gas tanks. Jonah was busy disconnecting the tanks, making sure a fire didn't start, when Casey stumbled out the door, not aware of her bloody hands and knees. She had been crawling through broken glass trying to get out of the cabin to safety.

Jonah's face had a look of horror as he grabbed her. "It's going to be all right. Let's get back inside and clean you up." He could see that Casey's wounds were only superficial. They calmed down, bandaged the wounds, and began to assess the situation.

"What was that?" Casey cried. "I've been in earthquakes before, but I've never experienced anything like that. I need to call my sons in St. Louis to let them know we're okay. Maybe they can find out what happened and where the epicenter was. It felt like it was right under my cabin."

"I was at Midway picking up a few groceries when it hit. I got here as fast as I could. See if your son knows what happened and I'll check your cabin over to make sure it's safe."

Casey had Bob on the phone trying to explain what happened. Bob found out almost immediately that it was an earthquake of magnitude 7.9 with the epicenter somewhere over by Paxton, which was not far from Slana. Bob told Casey he would call her back as more information became available, and to watch out for aftershocks; they would be coming.

Denali Fault: Highway Offset
Courtesy of the Geological Survey Department of the Interior /
USGS Photograph taken by Peter Haeussler

Jonah ran up the steps and into Casey's cabin. "I've got to go and check on the people out at Four Mile. The bridge may have damage. I'll pick up Maxx and Jed on the way."

"I'm going with you," Casey cried out. "My cabin is safe; I can clean this mess up later." They both left in Jonah's pickup, headed for Nebesna Road. Wide, deep cracks split the road, but it was passable and Jonah kept driving down the Cutoff, past trees that were broken off at their trunks. They were dazed by what had happened and feared the earth would crack open again. The rumble was gentle now beneath their feet. Casey had always thought of the earth as solid; she had always trusted the ground beneath her, but she feared she would never trust the ground below her feet again. As they turned on Nebesna Road, they saw that part of the dirt and gravel had disappeared. The terrain was not level; everything had shifted.

They came to Jed and Robyn's home, jumped out of the truck, and ran inside to find Robyn sitting on the floor crying. Casey stopped to comfort her while Jonah called out for Jed.

Jed heard Jonah from outside and cried out, "I'm on the roof. My chimney fell in and there's a hole in the rooftop."

Jonah ran to the back of their cabin and saw Jed picking up roof tiles and bricks from the broken chimney. Jonah brought him a tarp from a nearby shed and climbed the ladder to help Jed seal the damaged roof against the snow or rain.

Jonah told Jed they had to get out to Four Mile Road and check the bridge to make sure it was passable before anybody tried to drive over it. They were hoping to meet up with Maxx. They left on Jed's four-wheeler while Casey stayed with Robyn to help clean up the broken glassware and seal up two shattered windows. The earth continued to rumble, with aftershocks occurring every ten minutes. The women went to the root cellar only to find several pint jars of canned salmon shattered over the entire wooden floor. It was a mess, but they worked fast to clean it up. They were both afraid of another earthquake or a large aftershock that could trap them in the root cellar. When they were finished, they tacked a note to the front door, telling Jed and Jonah them they were checking on Linda Jo and the Post Office, which was only a quarter of a mile down the road.

Just as Jonah suspected, there was damage to the small bridge that the men had to cross to get to Four Mile Road. Maxx and Billy Joe were already there with Maxx's front loader reinforcing the bridge with large logs. The people who lived out past Four Mile Road would be stranded and not able to get to the Cutoff without the bridge. After an hour the four men managed to get the bridge reinforced, in spite of the constant aftershocks. It was strange, but they could set their watches to the frequency of the continued rumble. The aftershocks were every ten minutes, some a little stronger than others, but they persisted making everyone more nervous. Jonah and Jed left Maxx and Billy Joe to check on other residents down the road as the men drove towards Jonah's cabin. Jonah's place was intact with little damage, probably because it was made of logs and very small. They disconnected the propane and diesel tanks and headed back to Nebesna Road to find Casey and Robyn.

They caught up with the two women at Midway, where other Slana residents were discussing what the next plan of action would be. Adam and Katy had bottled water for sale on their shelves, which they decided to put aside to ration out when needed. Adam had already called the Red Cross in Anchorage to let them know that Slana residents needed help as soon as possible. As far as they could tell, nobody was really hurt, other than superficial cuts and bruises, but there was no water. All the wells were damaged and nightfall was coming quickly, with temperatures plummeting to ten below and colder, and the aftershocks continued to rumble every ten minutes.

Robyn started wailing, "There's going to be another one, I know it. It's going to come in the middle of the night and it will be too dark to see and we'll all freeze to death." Casey started to cry. Jed and Jonah looked at each other and knew it was going to be a long night with aftershocks continuing relentlessly every ten minutes; nobody was going to get any sleep. Jonah drove Casey home and they spent the next couple of hours cleaning up the cabin. The gas tanks were left disconnected, and for a late dinner they roasted hotdogs in Casey's woodstove. The cabin felt toasty warm as the fire burned in the stove, but the ground continued to rumble and both Casey and Jonah were afraid, not knowing what to expect.

It was a little awkward, but Jonah suggested that he stay with Casey for the night. They both came up with a plan that made them feel more comfortable. They put several blankets and a flashlight in Jonah's truck and left the truck keys, their boots and coats hanging on pegs in Casey's arctic porch. They were both concerned of another earthquake and wanted to make sure they could get out of the cabin safely if it occurred. They had two more flashlights sitting on the nightstand next to Casey's bed, and they slept in their warm clothes, ready to run if another earthquake hit. They would grab their coats, boots, and truck keys as they ran out the door to Jonah's truck, where they could quickly get warm and be safe. Casey and Jonah went to bed holding on to each other, feeling the aftershocks every ten minutes rocking the little settlement of Slana all night long.

Morning came, and it felt like neither Casey nor Jonah had slept a wink. The ground was still rumbling, but it was no longer every ten minutes, which was a big improvement for Casey. Casey went to the root cellar to bring up a five-gallon pail of water. That was one thing she didn't have to worry about. She had plenty of food stored in the cellar along with twenty-five gallons of water. Jonah went outside to turn on the propane tank so Casey could use the stove. She put a pot of coffee on and make a hearty breakfast for the two of them. He also turned the generator on, and luckily it was running fine, but the water pump for the well was damaged and there was no water. Jonah had learned yesterday after the earthquake hit that everyone's well gone dry. As far as they knew, there was no well that was working anywhere in Slana. But they did have fresh water from the river and the nearby streams, if they wanted to chip away the ice. After breakfast Casey and Jonah drove down to Midway to call a few residents in for a meeting. It was decided that they needed to get the wells up and running. They would tackle one well at a time. Midway's well was first in line for repairs. If they could fix Adam and Katy's well first, residents could come by the store and fill their water jugs. Slana Elementary School was second on their agenda. The school also had showers and a full kitchen. Maxx had the equipment and had previously dug wells for a couple of residents in Slana. He felt that the underground dirt had caved in during the earthquake; it was a possibility that the water pumps were not damaged, only displaced by the dirt. The only way to know for sure was to pull them up and see what parts might need to be replaced.

One at a time, they pulled up the water pumps and repaired what they could, making a list of parts that needed to be purchased from the dealer in Tok. As soon as the road became passable, someone would drive from Slana to get the parts. There was telephone contact with Anchorage and the outside world, but the roads were too damaged along the Tok Cutoff, so no one could get through. The road to Glennallen was open, but no one from Glennallen had the parts that were needed to repair the wells. Everyone just had to be patient and share what water they had. The Red Cross had told the townspeople that help was coming. It was going to take two or three days before help could be organized.

During that time the residents took care of each other and shared what they had, whether it was water, tools, or parts, and everyone worked together to repair whatever was damaged by the earthquake. After a couple of days the road to Tok opened up and Casey drove to Tok to get the well parts that were needed.

North of Slana around Mentasta had some of the worst damage. From the road, Casey could see a few buildings that were still standing but were not habitable. Casey stopped at Mentasta Lodge and learned that the Athabascans living in the village were all okay with only one injury, a broken arm. After the earthquake they all decided it would be safer for everyone to stay at their community center until damages could be assessed. Casey was impressed with the way everyone took responsibility for each other. Before Casey left the lodge, she asked if she could bring any supplies back from Tok. They seemed to have everything under control, so she left. From the lodge to the rest of the way into Tok was mostly a one-way road as workmen worked around the clock to repair the damage. At least it was open and they could get through. It took a few hours to get to Tok, a trip that normally would take a little over an hour. The damage along the way was devastating. Large trees were severed and broken off at the roots. There were sections of road that were ruptured which left heaves of asphalt and debris scattered over the terrain. A few cabins along the Cutoff were knocked off their foundations along with fuel tanks severed from their cribs. Casey finally made it to Tok and found that the man with the well parts had been waiting for her for the past couple of hours. After she picked up the parts, she bought a sandwich and several gallons of water from Three Bears Grocery Store and headed back down the Cutoff toward Slana. She hated to drive through the devastation again, but there was no other way. It was the only road back. It was obvious to Casey right where the fault line had ruptured, and it seemed odd that there was little damage anywhere else. It was like a powerful force had come along and just unzipped the earth.

It was dark by the time Casey pulled into the driveway at Midway. She had all the necessary parts that were so badly needed to fix the wells. The men were waiting and worked into the late night hours by the light powered by the Midway generator to get Adam and Katy's well fixed. They were determined that the people of Slana would have all the water they needed by tomorrow morning.

Chapter Fifteen: Getting Ready for the Holidays

The aftershocks continued to rumble the earth for the next few days. Their frequency had lessoned, but the townspeople were still on edge. The tremors came often and were unexpected, which made it hard for everyone to get back to a normal routine. The wells were all fixed and FEMA was taking samples of the water to make certain it was safe to drink. Jonah got his water from a nearby stream, and FEMA tested that water too. Jonah was told that underground springs had probably shifted during the earthquake.

The Red Cross showed up with bottles of water, and they were supportive to everyone. FEMA had sent inspectors to evaluate the damages in all of the homes and cabins. Everyone's home had been condemned due to the well-water situation, but the residents of Slana went one by one shoring up and repairing every home in Slana. Casey got to experience first-hand how an interdependent community worked. The people of Slana were amazing people, and Casey knew at that moment that she never wanted to return to suburban life in the lower forty-eight. She only hoped that one day her sons would also chose this lifestyle.

The Ahtna villages of Chistochina and Mentasta also worked together repairing damaged homes and roads. They were there for each other and nurtured each other through this very difficult time. Alaska had always been known to have earthquakes, but the Denali quake of 2002 was the worst recorded earthquake in history for the interior of the state. The people who lived in the Copper River Valley along the Tok Cutoff remembered the 1964 Earthquake that ravaged Anchorage and the surrounding areas, but no one in the Copper Basin had ever remembered an earthquake in the area with such magnitude as 7.9. The Denali Earthquake of 2002 was felt all over Alaska and was recorded to have been the worse earthquake of the year. The fault line ran from Denali National Park through Paxton then Mentasta and was felt all the way down to the gulf shore in Louisiana.

Seismologists were called to the area to study the aftermath of the earthquake to learn more about the Denali fault line. Research was done, and FEMA set up an informational meeting for all the residents that lived along the

Tok Cutoff. The meeting was held at the Slana Elementary School on a Saturday afternoon. Every able-bodied person showed up for the meeting, and the scientists answered questions the best they could. There was much concern about Mt. Sanford, an active volcano only fifty miles away, as the crow flies, that had begun sweltering, steam shooting out from its peak. It was obvious that the land formation had shifted, and everyone was afraid of what might happen in the future. The ground continued to rumble and it was very difficult to enjoy the peaceful way of life that everyone treasured. A suggestion was made at the meeting that the residents of Slana form a group at the small community center out just past Four Mile Road where residents could come together and share their fears and concerns. Somehow people were determined not to let the earthquake steal the peace and serenity of their lifestyle. The small neighbor group helped some residents to be able to vent their feelings.

People did what they could to relieve the tensions from the ongoing aftershocks. In the early days after the quake, even Jonah and Casey went into Anchorage for the weekend just to be able to feel solid ground beneath their feet. A couple of residents moved into Anchorage for a few months so they didn't have to experience the ongoing aftershocks. Casey often drove to Glennallen and spent afternoons sitting in her truck or walking in the town park because the earth felt solid. It felt odd to Casey that the ground felt stable only a couple of hours away from her cabin.

The rumbling got less and less as the days passed. Just as everyone would start to feel comfortable again, another strong aftershock would throw everyone into a panic. The residents of Slana were anxious for the holidays to arrive, not only to get their minds off their fears of the earthquake devastation, but to rekindle the town spirit.

Anna and Robyn came up with the idea of making Christmas cards for the holidays. There was no store from Tok to Glennallen that sold Christmas cards, so they would make their own. The community center in Slana was open to the townspeople, so Robyn contacted every woman she knew from Slana, Chistochina, and Mentasta to invite them to a card-making party. Katy spread the word through the Midway Store that they were planning a card-party event. She donated several different card stamps with ink pads of various colors that she had lying around the store. Casey had blank cards with envelopes and colored ink pens that she had stored away. Anna had an assortment of old wallpaper that could also be used as background for the cards. Several other women gathered whatever art supplies they could find around their homes. Five women from Mentasta planned to bring three crockpots full of reindeer chili, salmon chowder, and moose stew. The women from Chistochina were bringing spruce tree clippings, rose hips and dried berries to decorate the Christmas cards with. They were ready for a fun day of feasting and card making. The event was scheduled for a week before Thanksgiving; plenty of time to get their cards finished and mailed out to family and friends who lived outside. The party was scheduled for the Thursday before Thanksgiving, and the women were looking forward to making their holiday cards and enjoying each other's company. It would be a fun and practical thing to do, and they could hopefully forget about the earthquake devastation for at least a few hours.

River route on Slana River going towards the card party

Jonah plowing parking area

A few women from the three neighboring towns and villages showed up early Thursday morning to set up the tables and card supplies and to get everything ready for the party. A fire was started in the woodstove, and plenty of firewood was brought in to dry out. The generator was turned on to get the electric lights working and to heat up the crock pots full of homemade soups. Because of the seven inches of fresh snow that had fallen the night before, Jonah was even there plowing the gravel parking lot so the women could park their trucks and snowmobiles. Two women from Mentasta were coming with their sled dogs along one of the well-known trails from Mentasta to Slana. The weather was clear and cold at ten below. It was a beautiful morning and everyone was looking forward to the card-making party.

Twenty women arrived, and by ten o'clock, the community center was full of laughter and holiday cheer. Everyone was determined not to think or talk about the Denali earthquake. Hot chocolate and coffee were served, and everyone warmed up quickly. There were three large tables with card-making supplies available for everyone. Several women had never made cards before, so Casey, Anna, and Katy demonstrated ways they could use the card stamps and art supplies to make unique Christmas cards.

The spruce needles and dried berries were mostly used for a large poster that the two teachers, Robyn, and Casey worked on to advertise the upcoming Community Thanksgiving Dinner. The students who attended Slana School put on the dinner every year. It was a huge yearly event where most residents of Slana, including the surrounding areas, were invited to a full-course Thanksgiving dinner. The children worked hard the day before Thanksgiving, preparing several desserts in the school kitchen. They would also set up all the tables and chairs and would make holiday decorations for centerpieces on each table. Several turkeys and a couple of hams were provided by the school board, and families who were able brought side dishes for the Thanksgiving dinner.

While some of the mothers worked on the Thanksgiving poster, they talked about their children and what it meant for them to help prepare for the community dinner. It was the one time of the year that the children were active in serving their community in a very special way. Children in Slana were taught at an early age to give of themselves to each other and to care for the elderly who might not have a family to share Thanksgiving with.

It was mid-morning and the ground began to rumble again. The aftershock could not have been more than a 4.0, but they still rattled a few nerves. The festive mood quickly turned to doom as the Christmas cards began to move across the tables. Within a few seconds it was still again.

Casey frowned. "I wonder how long this is going to go on."

Trying to be optimistic, Robyn said, "Eventually it gets better. I was in the 1964 earthquake when it almost destroyed Anchorage. I was just a young girl, but I will never forget it. I promise; these little tremors will stop. I know it seems like the ground has been shaking forever, but it really hasn't been that long. It just wears on a person. I suppose we all take the ground beneath us for granted." Several of the women agreed.

It was a good time to stop their card making and have some lunch. Soon everyone forgot about the tremors and was having a good time sharing stories of past holiday seasons and how they celebrated them.

Martha, who lived out Nebesna Road shared her favorite Christmas story which took place when she was only five years old. The women gathered around in a circle with their hot soup and cocoa as Martha told her story.

"There were no cars or paved roads when I was a young girl, and my family traveled by sled-dog teams to neighboring villages along trails that were mostly used by the trappers. I remember my father having to break trail for the dogs when the snow was too deep for them to pull the sled. It was Christmas Eve and we still had several miles to go before we would be at my cousin's house. We had two dog teams carrying Christmas presents and holiday treats. Travel was so difficult back then, we always stayed wherever we went for at least a week. My mother drove one dog team and sled while my father drove the other. I remember how bitter cold it was, but my mother had me nestled under fur blankets amongst the many Christmas presents. My little brother was in my father's sled with all the holiday treats. We left early Christmas Eve and planned on arriving late that night. Back then there were no weather reports, and as you all know, the weather can change out here in a matter of minutes. Well, it did that Christmas Eve; a Chinook blew in from the south and my parents were blinded by the white-out conditions. Snow drifts made travel dangerous for the dogs and for us, but the dogs plowed on. I remember peeking out from my fur covers and asking my mother if we were almost there. She told me to get back under the covers and not to worry. It wasn't long after that that we stopped, but I knew we weren't at my cousins' yet. I poked my head out from under the warm covers and could vaguely see a grove of spruce trees and white birch. My mother told me to be still and to stay under the fur covers while she helped my father unhitch the dogs. I wasn't so afraid of the snow storm; we had been in similar situations before, but I didn't want to miss Christmas with my cousins. I only got to see them once a year.

"I huddled in the blankets for an hour, listening to the dogs barking and my parents scurrying around, and then my mother came for me. My father had a fire burning and was drying out spruce limbs. He had a pile of white birch bark that he fed the fire to keep it hot. The dogs were all tied down and nestled under the snow. My mother had a pot of moose soup warming by the fire and a basket of fry bread and berries. We had a Christmas Eve feast. After we were all fed, I helped my mother empty both sleds, and we slept for at least three or four hours. My mother and I slept in one sled while my father and little brother slept in the larger sled. The snow storm finally passed and we were back on the trail again, making our way to my cousins' cabin. It was Christmas morning and we were almost there.

"Smoke was coming from the chimney of my cousins' cabin as the dogs pulled our sleds into the yard. My uncle, a burly Alaskan sourdough, greeted us at the door with a gnarly old pipe in his mouth. Within minutes my three cousins were gathered around our dog sleds, helping us bring the presents and holiday treats into the cabin. It was Christmas morning and we were just in time to gather around the Christmas tree, which was decorated with homemade tin ornaments and dried berries that were strung and hanging on the tree. It was a family tradition for my aunt and my cousins to make special Christmas candles every year to be placed on the spruce tree that my uncle had cut down in the woods. My cousins were waiting patiently for us to arrive so we could put the candles on the tree. Within a few minutes all the presents were under the tree and the candles were lit. Our parents made us wait to open our presents. The dogs were fed while the women put the Christmas meal on the table. It was quite a feast, with a large moose rump roast and potatoes homegrown from their garden last spring. The cold-weather vegetables on the holiday table were also grown from my aunt and uncle's garden. There was plenty of homemade fry bread and berries for desert.

"After we finished our Christmas dinner, we sat around the Christmas tree catching up on the happenings of the past year. Finally it was time to open our presents. Of course, all of our Christmas presents were homemade. Remember, we had no access to a town where you could buy store-bought gifts. The gifts we made and shared with each other that Christmas day will always be dear to my heart. I got a pair of moose-hide mukluks that my uncle made. My aunt decorated them with colorful glass beads. My little brother got a fur comforter and a hat that was made from beaver and rabbit fur. We all got new moose-skin gloves that were also decorated with pretty beads. All the children got little fur yoyo's to play with, and my uncle gave my father a beaded rifle sheath for his .30-30 rifle.

"Every day we did daily chores and laughed and played. Twice we took the dogs out into the bush and checked my uncle's traps for animals that were needed for food to feed his family. My aunt would use the fur to make hats and gloves for all of us kids. Nothing was ever wasted. And that is one of my favorite Christmas memories."

The women appreciated Martha's Christmas story and felt fortunate that they too had the opportunity to live a subsistence lifestyle. Everyone was grateful that there were no more aftershocks that day. In the late afternoon the women returned to their homes with their homemade Christmas cards.

Chapter Sixteen: Delivering Thanksgiving Dinner to Slana Residents

Looking out through the kitchen window, Casey could see the wet snowflakes forming mounds of snow over the landscape. Heavy snow clung to the branches of the nearby spruce trees. There was already two feet of snow on the ground, and Casey wondered if it was going to snow all day. She decided to put her snowshoes on to walk out to the generator shed to start up the generator. She needed electricity to do the laundry and take a hot shower. Jonah was coming by that afternoon, and their plan was to deliver Thanksgiving hams and canned food and staples from the Alaskan Food Bank to surrounding neighbors who lived further back in the bush. They had fifteen families to deliver to. Jonah would be bringing his snowmobile and planned to meet Casey at the turnout near her cabin on the Cutoff. Casey would be in her one-ton four-wheel drive truck, keeping the Thanksgiving hams and boxes of food dry.

It didn't look like the snow was going to let up. They wanted to have the food boxes delivered by mid-afternoon before the dusk of late afternoon would turn to dark skies. The new fallen snow was a brilliant blanket of light that gleamed over the land in the moonlight, but Casey wasn't comfortable running on the frozen lakes and trails with the snowmobile. She trusted Jonah with her life, but still needed to feel more comfortable about the dangers that the harsh land could bring. She wanted to be back in her cabin by nightfall.

Since the earthquake, Casey often felt an uneasy feeling about the environment that surrounded her. Alaska was the most beautiful, serene place in the world and she didn't ever want to live anywhere else, but she also saw first-hand how the ground could just open up and swallow the quiet, peaceful landscape, leaving destruction and pain behind. It was something she was going to have to come to terms with.

Taking a hot shower was just what she needed. It was late morning and Jonah would be meeting her at the turnout in an hour. After finishing the laundry and eating a roast moose sandwich, she was ready to go. She grabbed her snowshoes from the arctic porch and went out to turn the generator off and start her pickup. The local news over the radio said the temperature was supposed to take a sharp drop to twenty below tonight. It would be good to get the food boxes delivered to where she could focus on the community Thanksgiving dinner that was being held at Slana Elementary School in only two days.

It was noon when Casey pulled into the turnout, and Jonah was waiting for her. There were ten easy deliveries, mostly on Nebesna Road and the Tok Cutoff, where they had easy access and the food boxes could be dropped off quickly. The other five locations were out Four Mile Road deeper in the bush. One family, which raised sled dogs, lived a couple miles further out in the woods and on a beautiful lake, which of course was frozen over this time of the year. Jonah had known them for years and often took care of their dogs when they went outside. That would be their last delivery, and if there was time they could visit for a little while.

The deliveries went well and people were happy to get the extra food, especially the ham, which was a rare commodity out in the bush. Everyone talked about the Thanksgiving dinner that was being held at the school, and they were looking forward to sharing their ham with the other residents. Arrangements for transportation had been made with every resident who didn't have a vehicle or a ride to the school. No one was forgotten or left out.

The snow finally began to let up during the last two deliveries, making travel easier and more pleasant. The temperature was beginning to drop as Jonah and Casey attached a sled to the snowmobile and headed out further in the bush with the last two boxes of food. It was a winter wonderland as they traveled along the trail with the fresh fallen snow blanketing the land. Casey was able to put the earthquake and the ongoing tremors out of her mind as they spun through the woods watching the snow fall from the limbs of the spruce trees. By the time they got to their last delivery, their weatherproof extremes were soaking wet from the fallen snow.

They pulled up to Ed and Kim's cabin and were greeted by at least twenty barking sled dogs. Kim and Ed appreciated the ham and box of food. After a cup of hot tea and a few minutes warming up by the fireplace, Kim asked Jonah and Casey if they wanted to go out and visit the dogs.

Casey smiled, excited. "I would love to see the dogs. Jonah has told me all about them and how Ed and he have gone mushing through the trails in the woods." They all walked outside to where the dogs greeted them with enthusiasm.

Ed laughed. "They're anxious to go for a run." He looked at Casey. "Have you ever been mushing before?"

Casey answered, "No, but Jonah has told me how much he enjoys taking the dogs for a run back in the woods along the trails."

"It will only take me a couple of minutes to hitch four or five of them up, and you can take them out over the lake for a quick run."

Jonah playing with Ed's dogs

Casey looked at Jonah and said, "Only a few minutes."

"If you don't mind getting home after dark, we can do it," Jonah answered

It took about thirty minutes for Kim and Ed to hitch up two teams of dogs. The plan was for Jonah to go out first with his team, and Casey would follow with her team of dogs. Jonah knew the dogs well and Ed knew they would obey him, but Ed was not sure how the dogs would react to an inexperienced musher. He didn't want the dogs to take off, sled and all, leaving Casey behind to walk back to the cabin.

"Sounds like a good plan," Casey said. With only fifteen minutes of instructions, Casey and Jonah were off with Jonah's team in the lead and Casey's dog team following close behind, obeying verbal commands. Only once did Jonah have to turn around and yell at Casey's dogs. Casey became more confident in handling her team and took off across the lake on her own. She loved it and wanted to head for the trails out in the woods, but she knew it would be dark soon, so they headed back to the cabin where Ed and Kim were waiting for them.

As Casey brought the dog team back, Ed was waiting to unhitch the dogs. Casey was beaming with excitement. "Can I come back and take the dogs for another run?"

"You bet, you can come back anytime you want," Ed answered, "The dogs are always anxious and ready to run. I'm always trying to get Jonah to get out here more and run my dogs, but since you moved to Slana he's been neglecting my dogs and spending his time with you; or so rumor has it. The dogs love him and I can see that they have taken a real shine to you, too."

Casey and Jonah laughed and Jonah said, "Yeah, guilty as charged, but looks like we can remedy this problem now that Casey has fallen for the dogs."

Ed had a sudden thought. "Why don't you and Casey take the dogs out for a week or so and go back into the mountains? There are plenty of good trails and even a couple of abandoned trapper cabins you could stay in if the weather decides to get ugly on you. There's nothing like going mushing in the middle of winter. It's an experience you'll never forget, Casey. You would be doing us a favor. Kim and I could go outside for a week to see her parents over the holiday season, and I would feel comfortable about leaving my dogs with the two of you."

Eagle at Ed's cabin looking for fish

Jonah looked at Casey and said, "What do you think? It's your call."

Casey thought for a minute and asked Jonah, "How well do you know the trails?"

"Ed and I have been over the trails many times," Jonah said. "I used to trap back in the mountains with my snowmobile on many of those trails. I know Ed's dogs well. I've been out here running them for the last three years. I'm comfortable with it if you are."

Casey smiled. "Yes, it would be a lot of fun, and Kim and Ed could go outside for the holidays."

It was dark now and the temperature was dropping. Jonah and Casey needed to get back to town before it got too late, but they were able to tell Kim and Ed that they would take the dogs out and care for them while they went outside. They would be in touch during the next couple of days to make the arrangements.

Casey and Jonah got back on the snowmobile and headed into the woods with the glimmering moon above lighting up the path for their short journey back to the Tok Cutoff. It had been a wonderful day, full of fun and adventure, and Casey was looking forward to returning to Kim and Ed's cabin to go mushing with Jonah into the Wrangell-St. Elias Mountains. Jonah suggested that they go by Duffy's Roadhouse to order a couple of hamburgers so they didn't have to fix dinner. Casey agreed, knowing it was the one place they could get a ground beef hamburger. Although they both loved moose meat, it was nice to have a regular hamburger for a change.

As they walked through the door at Duffy's, they spotted Jed and Robyn sitting at one of the booths, so they decided to join them. They were having a craving for beef hamburgers too. Jonah and Jed discussed the best trails to take for their trip into the Wrangell Mountains, while Casey and Robyn discussed plans for the Thanksgiving dinner at the school. Since Robyn was a teacher at Slana School, she was coordinating the dinner. Casey offered to help and come to the school to help the children prepare the meal for the Community Thanksgiving Feast.

****

The day before Thanksgiving was a busy one for Casey and Robyn. They were busy helping the children make table decorations for the dinner tables. Turkey dressing had to be made, and the children were scheduled to make special cut-out cookies with the substitute teacher during the afternoon. School work and recess were cancelled until the Thanksgiving Holiday was over and the children would return to school on Monday. Jonah and Jed went to Glennallen to pick up the turkeys and hams and brought them back to the school to be prepared. Even Jonah helped Casey stuff the three turkeys with all the trimmings and got the hams ready for the oven so they could be baked for tomorrow. The townspeople would be arriving tomorrow at 5 p.m. for their Thanksgiving dinner, and the school parking lot needed to be plowed again. Maxx was in charge of keeping the parking lot clear, which was a job due to the ongoing snowfall. At least the weather was not as cold as was predicted, so hopefully everyone young and old would come out for the holiday dinner.

This was Casey's first holiday season in Slana. She missed her sons back in St. Louis, but she knew they were planning a trip to see her next summer during hunting season. She felt fortunate to be accepted by the people who lived in the Alaska bush and remembered back when Maxx would call her a "cheechako." She had come a long way in the past few months and no longer called herself a "wanna-be bush woman." She had found a new home in Slana and had to admit that part of her joy was because of Jonah.

The townspeople began to show up at the school in the mid-afternoon on Thanksgiving Day. Everyone within a fifteen-mile radius showed up with side dishes that consisted of berries and breads along with a few casseroles made with reindeer, salmon, and moose meat. Casey was amazed at all the different dishes and planned to sample them all.

Soon everyone had arrived and was seated when the Thanksgiving prayer was said over the fine meal. People had picked up their plates and begun to form a food line when, once again, the earth began to rumble. It was a strong aftershock this time, a 5.5 at least, and the children began to scream and cry and dove under the tables for safety.

Casey and Robyn, both teachers, felt that the Denali earthquake affected the children the most. During school hours the children were often afraid to be away from their parents and seemed to be easily agitated. Finally the aftershock was over and parents and families comforted the children. Jonah noticed tears welling up in Casey's eyes and he went over to her to comfort her.

Casey cried in Jonah's arms and said, "Why, why does this have to hurt the children? Can't they have their Thanksgiving dinner in peace? They worked so hard for the past two days. It's not fair."

An old Ahtna woman, who had previously met Casey at Chistochina School, came up to her and said, "No need for you to fret. The children are strong, they will be good again. It is necessary for them to learn of such hardship. They grow strong, not only in body, but in spirit. It is good and necessary for children that live in the bush to have these lessons in life."

The old woman turned around and spoke out to the group. "We sing now and be grateful for this fine meal that has been prepared for us." The children came out from under the tables and began to sing with the old woman, and soon all was forgotten.

Jonah smiled at Casey and said, "That's a wise old woman. We all need to remember her words. There is no land like the Alaskan Frontier, but at times it can be very unforgiving."

"Or it can be the most beautiful, serene place in the world. It's however you look at it on any given day." Smiling, Casey reached for Jonah's hand and said, "Happy Thanksgiving."

Chapter Seventeen: Dog Mushing for the Holidays

Looking out her cabin window, Casey wondered if it would ever stop snowing. So far it had been a fairly mild winter, with several days reaching temperatures up into the low thirties, causing foot after foot of snowfall. It was two weeks before Christmas and Casey was anticipating her holiday dog mushing trip with Jonah. They were leaving in two days for the back-country trails out past Four Mile Road. Jonah had already spoken with Bet, the forest ranger, at Nebesna Ranger Station, to give her an idea of the areas of the park they would be traveling in and the dates they planned to be gone. Whenever traveling in wilderness areas, it is always customary to let someone know when you plan on leaving and when you plan on returning and to always check in as soon as you get back, or a search and rescue team would be called in to find your missing party.

Jonah and Casey planned to stay out on the trails for only five days and spend the last few days, including Christmas day, at Ed and Kim's cabin caring for the dogs and running them out on the lake and in the nearby woods until they got back from visiting family in the lower forty-eight.

It was a brisk, windy morning when Jonah and Casey set out for Ed and Kim's cabin on Jonah's snowmobile, pulling a sled-full of clothes and supplies for their winter trip into the back country with the dogs. They couldn't think of a better place to spend their Christmas holiday. Because they each had their own dog team and sled, they would have enough room for all their camping supplies and food for themselves and for the dogs. After a full day of instructions from Ed on caring for the dogs and taking care of his cabin, Ed and Kim were ready to drive to Anchorage and fly outside for the holidays.

Finally Jonah and Casey were alone and decided to build a warm fire in the wood stove. They each had a bowl of salmon chowder for dinner as they sat by the warm, glowing stove discussing their plans and looking forward to the next morning, when they could leave with the dogs for the back country. They were bringing the necessary tools for repairing the sleds and harnesses for the dogs. Their camping equipment included a tent, stove pipe and damper with poles, blankets and ponchos, and sleeping bags. They had a camp cook kit that included candles and matches and all the necessary cooking supplies. They were well prepared for bad weather with a wool suit of clothes and extra wool socks and mitts. They also packed lightweight clothes and wind pants and a parka. They included several pairs of booties for the dogs. They were prepared for any weather that Mother Nature decided to send them.

It was early morning and the moon was brilliant in the sky, shining over the snow-covered terrain. The dogs were up and ready to run. Jonah looked over the canines and chose nine yelping sled dogs for Casey, with Emma running as the lead dog. Jonah had a larger sled with a heavier load, so they harnessed eleven restless, anxious dogs with Bruiser as the lead dog. They had gone over their checklist of everything they needed, and they were packed up and ready to get on the trail. The dogs yapped and howled and were difficult to hold back.

"I've never seen these dogs so excited," Jonah called over the noise of the dogs. "I'm going to take off and run about a quarter-mile ahead of your team, then bring your team up the rear, but keep some distance between us until they get used to running with my team."

Casey yelled, "I'll hold them back, go ahead, we're ready."

Bruiser took off like lightening with the other dogs following. They were off running down the bank through the spruce trees and heading straight over the lake, which glistened in the moonlight with a bright sheen of slick ice beneath their paws. Casey gave Emma her lead while the dogs leaped forward and were on the trail like a flash. After about twenty minutes, both dog teams settled down to a steady trot and Casey was able to catch up with Jonah without the dogs wanting to fight or race ahead on the trail.

Jonah getting the harnesses

Jonah and Casey taking the dogs on the trail

The moon had begun to disappear below the horizon when the sky turned to a soft gray. Clouds were beginning to appear while snowflakes gently fell along the trail and covered the back country. It was so quiet and peaceful as they traveled along a trapper's trail that lead down past the Slana River and onto one of the creek beds. They passed a grove of aspen trees and watched a cow moose and her two calves feeding off nearby willows. The dogs were in their glory to be out in the wild and running a comfortable, steady pace. There were a couple of steep hills to climb, and one in particular that Emma balked at, stopping and turning around to look at Casey as if to say, "You need to get off that sled and help push this load up this hill." Casey knew what Emma was trying to communicate, and she jumped off the sled and pushed it up the hill, lightening the load for her dogs.

Jonah noticed they were lagging behind and yelled back at Casey, laughing, "What's the matter with you ladies? Are you tired already?"

Casey looked up and said with a sneer on her face, "You have two more dogs on your team than I do. I think it's time to take a break and have some lunch."

Jonah agreed but didn't admit that he too was ready to take a break. He called back to Casey, "There's a nice grove of white birch over to the left of the trail, just beyond that curve. Why don't we stop there for a break?"

Both Casey and Jonah hollered out to their dogs, "Gee," and their teams took a sharp left and quickly came up on the grove of birch trees. They slowed their teams down and signaled their dogs to stop. Pulling out their anchors from the side of their sleds, they shoved them down under the snow deep into the earth, letting the dogs know that it was time to stop and they had better not get any ideas about running off. Jonah spotted a couple of dead birch trees and pulled his hatchet from his sled. Soon they had firewood to build a fire to warm up. Casey took a large pot from her sled and filled it with snow to put on the camp fire. She added two nice-sized pieces of frozen, dried salmon and threw them into the pot to make some salmon broth for the dogs. As it began to melt down, Casey and Jonah checked every dog's paws to make certain none of them had any injuries or had lost their booties. The dogs began to howl and bark when they smelled their salmon brew. Jonah took each dog a large cup of broth and salmon pieces for extra energy and to warm them up. After they drank their warm broth, they decided to lie down in the snow for a short nap while Casey and Jonah had dried salmon and pilot bread for lunch. Casey pulled out a hot thermos of water and some of Jonah's special herb tea, and they sat by the warm fire drinking tea and enjoying each other's company. After an hour they decided to get back on the trail. They smothered the campfire with snow and packed up their belongings. As soon as they pulled the sled anchors out of the ground, the dogs were up, howling and barking and ready to run. They headed back deeper into the bush but decided to stay on the old trapper's trail, where Jonah was familiar with the hill. The woods were silent with only the sound of the sleds moving across the snow. At one point a snow-white rabbit crossed the trail within a hundred feet of the dogs and Bruiser took off like a flash, chasing him down a hill and dragging the other dogs behind him. Jonah yelled words of profanity at him and held firm on the sled brake to no avail. There was just no stopping Bruiser and the team of dogs. A half-mile down a steep hill, Bruiser made a sharp right turn, dumping Jonah, the sled, and all the supplies into the snow. Casey led Emma and her dogs off the trail and followed Jonah, trying to catch up. Jonah's parka was soaking wet along with all the supplies he was carrying in his sled. It was nearly 3 p.m. and it would be dark in an hour. The sky was beginning to clear and the temperatures were dropping, and they both knew they needed to gather up the supplies and get back on the trail as soon as possible and find some shelter. Within a few minutes they had the dogs hitched up and were back on the trail looking for a thick grove of trees so they could set up camp. They were lucky and found a nice grove of spruce trees and alders only a quarter of a mile down the trail. They quickly staked out the dogs for the night, and both Casey and Jonah cut down a couple of dead alders for a fire. Jonah knew he could go back later to cut more firewood after they got camp set up.

Casey found a hatchet in her sled bag and cut down several spruce boughs to use to level out the ground beneath their tent. A space blanket would be placed over the boughs, which would help to insulate them from the frigid snow beneath their tent. The boughs would provide a soft, dry mattress to lay their sleeping bags on. Jonah pitched the tent while Casey cut more wood for the fire and started drying out Jonah's parka along with one of the sleeping bags that had gotten tossed into the snow along with the rest of their gear that also needed to be dried out. The weather was beginning to worsen, and it appeared that they were going to get more snow. Casey and Jonah tied the canvas sled tarp to a couple of trees up above their tent to shelter them from the snow that would fall during the night. They even had a small camp stove with a damper if it got too cold. Their shelter was complete, and now they could focus on getting the dogs and themselves some dinner.

Jonah fed the dogs salmon mixed with a vitamin supplement that was part of their daily diet. Casey prepared hot instant soup and added frozen cheese to it. She opened a can of salmon, which they ate with crackers. The dogs were anchored down for the night, and they curled up in a bed of snow and slept through the evening. Jonah and Casey made hot tea with spruce needles and ate store-bought cookies for dessert. They held each other close as they sat under the tarp by the campfire and watched the snow fall over the land.

Morning came with a gentle breeze blowing through the spruce trees, awakening Jonah and Casey. They had been warm and comfortable in their sleeping bags in spite of the snowfall during the night. Their spruce bough mattress kept them amazingly warm, and they were reluctant to leave their tent and start a fire. When Jonah stepped out, the dogs woke immediately and began to bark for some breakfast. Casey made hot oatmeal and coffee for breakfast while Jonah fed the dogs. By mid-morning they were packed up and mushing along the trail toward an old abandoned trapper's trail that had not been used for several years.

It was a clear, cold day with temperatures rising to ten degrees. The air was quiet and still, and the only thing that could be heard was a few ravens cawing in the distance. Jonah and Casey continued to run their dog teams for another two hours before they ran across an old, abandoned trapper's cabin. It was a good time to stop for lunch and check the dogs. They anchored their sleds and walked inside the dilapidated cabin, which held an old wood stove, a table and chairs, and a couple of old cots. They decided to leave most of their camping gear in the cabin, have a quick snack, and return to the trail. The day began to warm as the hours passed. The trail took them alongside rocky creeks that eventually lead them back to the Slana River. The dogs ran down the center of the river, not taking any chances to get too close to the river's edge where the ice might be too thin to run on. As they came to a bend in the river, they came upon a small herd of caribou grazing by the riverbank. The caribou looked up, lifting their large racks of antlers, and just watched Jonah and Casey pass by. Shortly after spotting the caribou, Casey and Jonah decided to take a break and let the dogs rest before they circled back to the old trapper's cabin, where they planned to spend the night.

Emma and Bruiser trotted back along the river trail, leading their faithful followers at a steady pace. The dogs were well rested after their break and scampered along the trail with their unfurled tails across their backs. They did love to run, especially when the snow wasn't too deep. Jonah called out to Bruiser "haw" and the dogs took a sharp right turn into the woods, with Emma and her team scurrying to keep up. Casey gave her dogs the lead but stayed close behind Jonah and his team. The dusk of the late afternoon would be disappearing soon, and they wanted to get back to the trapper's cabin, where they had left most of their gear. Nightfall was approaching when they spotted a large, dark figure beneath a grove of birch trees. At first Casey thought it might be a moose resting in the grove, but as she got closer Casey saw that it was a man and a snowmobile turned over on its side.

Jonah got there first, anchored his team, and ran over to the man. Casey came up and settled the dogs down so Jonah could tend to the injured man.

The man spoke in a weak but relieved voice. "My name's Ken, and I've been here for the past three hours praying someone would come along and spot me. I hit a tree stump just under the snow line and broke a skid on my snow machine. It threw me about twenty feet and I landed up against these trees. My foot is either broken or maybe it's a bad sprain. Either way, I can't walk."

"We need to get you out of this wind and snow and tend to that ankle," Jonah said. "There's an old trapper's cabin about two miles from here, where we planned to spend the night. We dropped most of our gear at the cabin, so there's room for you in Casey's sled. I can come back and look at your snowmobile tomorrow and figure out what to do."

Jonah and Casey quickly arranged their supplies and made room for Ken in Casey's sled. Emma and Bruiser sensed a problem and went into an alert mode: they were ready to run.

When Ken was covered in a blanket, lying in Casey's sled, she called out to Jonah, "We're ready to go, we're burnin' daylight."

Jonah gave a loud command to Bruiser and both teams were off and running. There was no time to waste; nightfall was upon them, with no moon to guide the way back to the old cabin. Bruiser sensed the urgency and raced down the trail, instinctively knowing where to go. It was pitch black when they reached the cabin. They were in luck—the previous guest had left two piles of firewood. Casey built a fire in the wood stove, which warmed up the cabin almost immediately. Jonah helped Ken into the cabin, where he sat by the fire warming up. Casey made up some warm broth for Ken to drink while she started to fix a late dinner, while Jonah checked the dog's paws and anchored them down for the night. Jonah gave each dog an extra hunk of salmon along with extra strokes of gratitude for getting them back to the cabin so quickly.

When Jonah came inside, Casey had a hot meal of reindeer sausage and pancakes ready for everyone to feast on. After dinner Jonah looked at Ken's injured foot and thought he probably had a bad sprain. The three of them bunked down for the night after a long, active day on the trails.

Jonah was up early the next morning and tended to the dogs while Casey fixed them hot broth with dried salmon chunks. The swelling in Ken's foot had gone down and he was able to stand on it. Casey made up some oatmeal for breakfast and a thermos of hot coffee for Jonah. He wanted to take the dogs back to where Ken's snow machine was and take a better look at the broken skid.

Jonah said to Ken while he was just finishing up his oatmeal, "I think I can fix that broken skid if I strip down one of these birch trees and cut it into a makeshift ski. As soon as it's daylight, I'll take a few tools and head back to your snow machine with the dogs."

Jonah cut down one of the birch trees outside the cabin and worked at stripping off the bark and splitting it down the center with his hatchet. Ken worked at taking off the knots on the soft wood until it was finally smooth. As soon as it was light, Jonah took some duct tape and wire from his supplies and hitched up the dogs with Bruiser in the lead. He took his bowie knife and hatchet to cut the wood if necessary to fasten it on the broken skid. The wire and duct tape should hold the skid in place until Ken could get back to Porcupine Creek, where his cabin was. Casey rode in Jonah's sled and would bring Bruiser and the dog team back while Jonah rode the snowmobile back to the trapper's cabin; that is, if he could get the makeshift wooden skid to work. Casey was amazed at the way Jonah could fix things with whatever was available that he could find out in the bush.

It took Jonah over an hour to fix the skid and tie it down to the snow machine. After taking a ten-minute test drive, he felt certain the wooden skid would stay on the snow machine. Casey drove the dog team back to the old cabin while Jonah rode the snowmobile. As they pulled up to the cabin, Ken was standing in the doorway, happy to see them both and even happier to see that his snow machine was running. Ken reassured Jonah and Casey that his foot felt much better and he could make it back to his cabin without their assistance. He thanked the two of them as he drove his snow machine down the trail toward the Tok Cutoff.

Jonah and Casey decided to stay at the old trapper's cabin for the next two nights and took day runs with their dog teams.

Jonah taught Casey how to ice fish on one of the nearby lakes. They caught six burbits and two white fish and had quite the feast for dinner that night, and even made some fresh fish broth for the dogs. One afternoon while they were mushing on one of the nearby river trails, Emma and her dog team came up on a grove of dead birch trees. Casey and Jonah spent the afternoon cutting down the trees and dragging them back to the cabin, where they split wood off and on for the next couple of days. When it was time to get back to Ed and Kim's cabin, they had gathered enough firewood for the next couple of visitors who might stumble along and find the old trapper's cabin. Casey also left a note and a couple pints of canned salmon for the next occupant.

Jonah and Casey had a wonderful holiday vacation out in the bush with the dogs, but they were both happy to be getting back to Ed and Kim's cabin. On their way back Jonah cut down a nice looking spruce tree that they decorated for Christmas. It was Casey's first Christmas in the Alaska bush, and she was happy to spend it with Jonah and the sled dogs.

Chapter Eighteen: Life Cycle of the Salmon and the Fish Wheel

Winter was a beautiful time of the year in the Copper River Valley, and Casey had a hard time deciding which season she liked best, winter or getting ready for winter. It had been almost a year since she moved to Slana, leaving the lower forty-eight behind her. Since the holidays had passed, she and Jonah got their snowshoes out and went for long walks in the woods. Sometimes they would leave early in the morning, drive out past Glennallen to Eureka, and ride the mountain trails on Jonah's snow machine. Winter was a time for fun and relaxation. Come spring, Casey was planning on getting her own snowmobile and four-wheeler. She knew Alaska was to be her permanent home. Even though Casey found plenty to do during the long winter months, she found herself waiting for spring, even though it would bring a lot of hard work. It had been a fairly mild winter, which left her with more than enough firewood to carry her into spring. There would be plenty of cold spring evenings to where they could invite a few neighbors and have bonfires by the river.

Breakup would be happening soon, when the thick river ice would crackle and break apart while making its way down the Slana River. Soon after, it would be time to plow up her garden space and plant her seedlings. Casey was planning on putting her garden in around mid-June, as soon as she was fairly certain there would be no more frost. Most of all, Casey was waiting for the salmon to make their run from the ocean up the Copper River and into the nearby tributaries to spawn and lay their eggs.

In early June, Jonah called Casey. "It's time, there are reports that the salmon are starting to make their way up the Copper River. They'll be here in a week or so, and it's time to put the fish wheel in. Maxx is bringing his front loader, and Jed and I are going to help him slide the wheel into the river. It will take us a couple of hours to get it set up and anchored into the river bank. Do you want to meet us at the old road house on Nebesna Road and watch us put it in?"

Casey had been waiting all year for the salmon to start running. "Yes, of course, and maybe Robyn and Anna will come too. I'll give them a call." Plans were made and the three women met at Midway to drive down together and watch them put the fish wheel into the river. When Casey arrived at Midway she found that the word had gotten out and the whole town knew that the wheel was going in that afternoon. They were making bets on when the first salmon would arrive and meet its fate in the fish wheel.

Everyone in Slana who had a subsistence permit had signed up with Bet at the Nebesna Ranger Station to use the fish wheel. Maxx actually owned the wheel but shared it with anyone with a permit who was a resident of Slana. A family was allowed to take three hundred fish during the salmon season, which was plenty of fish to be canned, smoked, or dried out and made into salmon jerky. Salmon was a main staple for the residents. They were not allowed to make a profit by selling the fish, but were allowed to give it away. Each subsistence permit holder would take a twenty-four hour turn on the fish wheel and gather whatever fish got swept up by the wheel. Each permit holder would have a number and would need to post it on a tree to let people know who got the fish on that particular day. The system worked well, and everyone got all the salmon they needed or wanted during the season.

The fish wheel was an amazing contraption, with a paddle wheel on one end and a basket on the other end. The swift current from the Copper River would push the paddle and turn the wheel, and the fish would get caught in the large basket. As the basket turned on the wheel, it would throw the salmon into a large box at the base of the fish wheel. Whoever was scheduled on the fish wheel on that particular day would only have to collect the fish from the box, usually three or four times a day.

"There isn't a lot of sport to this kind of fishing," Jonah said, "but it's very efficient in feeding your family for the year. It's also fun to do sport fishing like we did when we went ice fishing a couple of months ago."

Casey agreed. "There's something for everyone in this state, and I enjoy it all."

Jonah smiled. "Why don't we sign up for our days on the wheel together? We can help each other clean and can fish and get twice as much done in a shorter period of time; plus it will be twice as much fun."

Casey laughed. "Yeah, that's a great idea. You can skin and clean the fish, and I'll cut them up and can them over at my cabin."

Jonah liked the idea. "We can also dry some out for salmon jerky and smoke some to be canned in your canner too. We'll have plenty of salmon this winter." Casey agreed and they picked out their days on the wheel with Maxx, and then reported it to Bet.

The salmon finally arrived, and Maxx took the first couple of days on his fish wheel. Jed and Robyn were next. It was a good salmon run, and it looked like there would be plenty of fish for everyone. Jonah was on the wheel next and Casey was looking forward to pulling the fish from the box. It was such an easy way to fish. It was early morning when they checked the salmon box, and there were eight large, red sock-eye salmon and one huge king salmon in the box.

Jonah cried out to Casey, "We've got nine big ones, they're alive and fighting. Can you bring me my wooden club?"

They kept slipping out of Jonah's hands, so Casey joined him to try and grab the fish while Jonah clubbed them to their death. It wasn't quite as easy as Casey had thought it would be. Then again, nothing ever was out in the bush. Their huge fish pail was soon full of bright, red-orange, beautiful salmon meat. The seagulls began to fly around the wheel, begging for scraps of salmon guts. Casey could see three bald eagles high up in the trees, observing the show while Jonah kept processing the fish. Casey threw the salmon waste up on a nearby rock for the seagulls to feast on and watched to see if the eagles would fly down for some breakfast. They were much too skittish for that to happen. Casey and Jonah carried the heavy fish pail to Jonah's pickup and heaved it up and into the truck bed.

Climbing into his truck, Jonah said, "We have one more stop to make before we can take the fish to your place and refrigerate them, and that's Autel Creek. Autel Creek is where everyone takes their fish to rinse them off good before you take them into your house for canning. We do need to keep a lookout for bear. They can smell the salmon a mile away and like to hang out at the creek sometimes. Will you reach into the back and grab my rifle?"

Jonah and Casey at the Fish Wheel

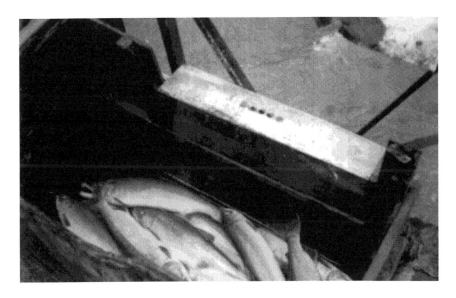

A full box of fish

Casey frowned, grabbed the rifle, and sarcastically said, "Oh that's just great, that's just what I need—another run-in with a bear."

Jonah smiled. "Don't worry, if any bears are hanging around and they start to approach us, we leave the fish and hightail it out of there. The rifle is just a precaution." Jonah laughed. "We know where we can get more fish. The bears have to eat too."

Casey didn't see the humor in Jonah's remark. "Yeah, Yeah. There's just some things I'll never get used to, and one of them is bears."

As they turned down the dirt road to Autel Creek, Casey could hear the gentle gurgling of water passing over the creek bottom. Aspen, white birch, and alders grew thick along the bank of the creek. Jonah backed his pickup right to the edge of the water while Casey got out of the truck armed with Jonah's rifle. She wasn't taking any chances. Jonah began rinsing the fish with the clear water in the creek.

Grizzly bear near Autel Creek

Casey, enjoying the cool breeze from the creek, suddenly looked up and saw a grizzly and two cubs wandering down the creek bed toward their pick up and their fish. The bears were about six hundred feet from the truck when the mother bear reared up on her hind legs to get a better look at what Jonah was doing. Casey was sure that the bears smelled the fish.

Casey said in a panicked whisper, "Jonah, there are bears in the creek coming toward us. They smell our fish."

Jonah jumped up and grabbed his rifle from Casey, saying in a low voice, "They look like they're just checking us out. I don't think they're going to charge us, but you're right, they do smell our fish. Hurry, let's grab our fish and throw them in the back of the truck. We need to get out of here before that sow and her cubs decide to change their minds."

They were in the truck in less than fifteen seconds and very relieved to be headed toward Nebesna Road away from Autel Creek and the bears. They pulled into Casey's driveway, went inside, and finished rinsing off the fish. Casey cut the salmon into six-inch strips and placed them on a large platter to be refrigerated. Then they returned to the fish wheel to gather more fish.

It had been three hours since they checked the fish wheel. As they were driving down Nebesna Road, they made a sharp right turn at the old road house, where the dirt road would lead them to the Copper River where the fish wheel was churning away. When they arrived at the wheel, they walked out onto the wooden planks and found a full box of salmon. Casey and Jonah worked fast at getting the salmon out of the box and immediately started gutting and cleaning the fish. After they took the fish from the box, they counted fifteen red sock-eye salmon. Next they left the salmon roe and guts on the nearby rock and drove to Maxx's cabin, where he had salmon drying poles and a homemade salmon smoker set up in his yard. These fifteen salmon would be dried and smoked and saved for the long winter months ahead.

When they arrived at Maxx's home, Jonah showed Casey the salmon smoker that Maxx had made out of an old abandoned stainless steel refrigerator. Prime cuts from the salmon's belly were sliced and laid on shelves in the salmon smoker, while the deep pan at the bottom of the smoker smoldered with coals burning hickory wood. The finished product was a delicious dried piece of salmon with a smoked hickory flavor. Some of the salmon were also smoked for a shorter time and given to Anna to be cut into chunks and processed in pint jars in her canner. Maxx and Anna ate salmon year round, just as all the people in Slana did that held a subsistence permit. A few of the salmon were cut and sliced and hung over long salmon poles to dry out in the sun. It was good meat for the many sled dogs in the community as well as good fish meat to be stored in a cache for the cold winter months ahead.

Another couple hours passed as they continued to process the fish, and then Jonah commented to Casey, "I guess it's time to get back to the fish wheel to see how many more fish we have in the fish box."

Casey, after observing all of the processed salmon, said, "Yeah, we can't stop now; the wheel is still turning and churning and throwing fish into the fish box. This is going to go on for our whole twenty-four hours on the fish wheel."

Jonah laughed. "It's a mighty hard day of work, I'll admit to that, but our last trip to the wheel is around nine o'clock, and then whoever is on the fish wheel tomorrow can have the night's catch when they show up tomorrow morning. You will be amazed at how fast our stash of fish will disappear this winter."

Casey knew that it just wasn't about picking the salmon out of the fish box, cleaning and processing each fish. Tomorrow she and Jonah would be putting all the reddish-orange salmon meat in all the glass pint jars and processing every jar in the canner.

Casey laughed and said to Maxx and Jonah, "Oh yeah, I forgot about the only two seasons in Alaska, winter and getting ready for winter. Who ever made that up sure knew what they were talking about, but if I had to be honest, I would never want to live any other way or in any other place other than Alaska."

Jonah smiled. "Do you want to make one more run to the fish wheel, and then I'll buy you a hamburger at Duffy's Roadhouse?"

Casey laughed. "Sounds like a bribe to me, but I'll take you up on that hamburger." They climbed into Jonah's truck and drove toward the old roadhouse on Nebesna Road to make another run for more salmon.

When they got to the fish wheel and looked into the fish box, there were seven more salmon to gut and then rinse off at Autel Creek. Casey was hoping the mama bear and her two cubs would not be lingering, looking for a dinner meal. Casey was relieved when they drove down the dirt road and backed the truck up near the edge of the creek bed. There were no bears. After a few minutes they were finished rinsing off the salmon, and they drove down the Tok Cutoff to drop the fish off at Casey's cabin and make their way to Duffy's for a hamburger. They ran into Jed and Robyn and joined them for dinner and an hour of nice conversation. Jed and Robyn were scheduled on the fish wheel for tomorrow and were looking forward to grilling some nice fresh salmon steaks. Casey suggested that Jed and Robyn stop by her cabin. She and Jonah would do the grilling, and they could have a bonfire after dinner if everyone wasn't too exhausted. It was to be a busy week with canning fish and then tilling the garden and having it ready to plant by mid-June.

Casey smiled to Jonah. "We're burnin' daylight again. We better get down to that fish wheel before the fish overflow the fish box."

Jonah laughed. "Burnin' daylight? What's that all about? We're burnin' daylight twenty-four hours a day up here during the summer months. It's impossible to run out of daylight till winter."

Casey chuckled. "And it's impossible to run out of work that needs to be done. If I've learned anything about living out in the bush, it's that the work is never really done. It's an uphill battle to get everything done by fall, so we can't be burnin' daylight."

Jonah laughed and looked at Jed and Robyn. "She's quite the slave driver. The salmon are calling her; we gotta run."

Casey and Jonah were off and headed one more time down the Cutoff, making a left turn onto Nebesna Road and then a sharp right at the old roadhouse and onto the dirt road that led down to the fish wheel. Much to their surprise, there were only two salmon in the fish box.

Jonah called out to Casey in an eager voice, "We get to burn a little daylight—only two of them made it up the river into the wheel."

It was nearly nine o'clock when Casey and Jonah decided to take a break and sit on the bank of the Copper River, listening to the paddle wheel turn the big fish wheel and watching the sun drop below the horizon.

Casey felt the gentleness of Jonah's arm slip around her and thought, *Our journey living in the bush of Alaska is like the journey the salmon make every year up the Copper River.* She thought about how the salmon are born in the tributaries that branch off the mighty Copper River and make their long, dangerous journey out to the sea. They live and grow in the ocean, threatened by predators for a few short years until they're called back to their original nesting grounds to lay their eggs and eventually die where their journey first began. They fight hard, swimming upstream all the way until they make the full cycle of their journey.

She realized how like the salmon the people of Alaska were. In the circle of life, they struggled to survive in an untamed wilderness, often surrounded by predators and fighting against the current of the outside world that doesn't always understand what the struggle is all about.

Casey turned to Jonah and looked deep within his eyes and said, "What makes us different from the salmon in this river is we have the ability to love and care for one another through our own journey of life."

Jonah turned to Casey as he took her in his arms. "I am glad we are traveling that journey together."

Glossary

Arctic Room   A room to step into from outside to take one's winter gear off and shields the rest of the house from the arctic winter air

Bob Tail   A word used to describe a tractor traveling without a 53 ft trailer

Break up   When the winter ice on the rivers break apart in the spring

Bunny Boots   Well insulated boots to keep one's feet warm up to -30*

Bush   Out in the back country, usually with no road access.

Cache   A small storage room, usually built on stilts high off the ground to store meat to keep away from animals

Camp Robber   A gray jay, known to be a scavenger of people food

Cheechako   A newcomer or greenhorn

Chinook   A warm wind usually blowing from the south

Outside   A word used to describe a place that is outside of Alaska

Slough   An area where a small section of a river becomes a pond and eventually flows back into the river

Ahtna Language

Trees and Plants

Alder	k'es	(*kess*)
Birch	k'ey	(*kay*)
Cottonwood	t'eghes	(*the-wess*)
Grass	tl'ogh	(*kloe*)
Leaf	c'et'aan'n	(*keh-tawn'n*)
Pussy willow	dahliggaaye'	(*daw-lee-guy-yeh*)
Spruce	ts'ebael	(*tse-bale*)
Spruce bark	c'elaats'l	(*gil-a-tan*)
Spruce cone	lacduuy	(*lock-doo-ee*)
Spruce gum	dzaex	(*zak*)
Spruce needle	'e laggade'	(*eth-la-god-deh*)
Spruce root	xey	(*he*)
Willow	k'ey'	(*kay-t*)

Birds

Arctic Loon	ts'albaet	(*t-sell-bat*)
Bufflehead	tuhtsedl	(*too-sed-el*)
Camp robber	takalbaey	(*tok-all-bay*)
Canada Goose	xax	(*hok*)

143

Canvasback	ndzeli	(*n-zell-ee*)
Chickadee	ne'iine'	(*neh-ee-neh*)
Common Loon	tadziil	(*tad-zeeth*)
Ducks (all)	dats'eni	(*dot-sen-ee*)
Eagle	tuudi	(*too-dee*)
Magpie	tsakatniigi	(*chak-at-nee-gee*)
Mallard	t'aaycogh	(*tie-choe*)
Owl	besiin	(*bess-seen*)
Raven	tsaghani	(*sa-gaw-nee*)
Robin	suux	(soot)
Seagull	nalbaey	(*nall-bay*)
Snowbird	ggaex	(*ga*)
Swallow	dzuuts	(*joots*)
Swan	taggo	(*tag-gose*)
Willow Ptarmigan	lacbae	(*lock-ba*)
Woodpecker	cenc'kadi	(*ken-kes-kaw-dee*)

Fish

Burbit (Ling Cod)	ts'aann	(*chan-ya*)
Dolly Varden	ts'engastlaeggee	(*chen-gast-lag-eh*)
Grayling	tsabaey	(*cha-bay*)
King Salmon	luk'ece'e	(*thloo-kek-eh*)

Lake Trout	baet	(*bat*)
Minnows	'ul'uli	(*koolth-kool-lee*)
Pike	c'ulgaadzi	(*kool-gad-zee*)
Pin nose	kasten'	(*kass-ten*)
Salmon	luk'ae	(*thloo-ka*)
Sucker	tats'ade	(*tat-sod-eh*)
Whitefish	luux	(*thlook*)

Berries

Blueberries	gigi	(*gih-gee*)
Cranberries	xay gige'	(*hie gih-geh*)
Crowberries	naht'aezi	(*na-taz-zee*)
Currant	danihnuuy	(*don-nee-noo-ee*)
Raspberry	denc'oggo'	(*den-koe-go*)
Rosehips	ncuus	(*n-quse*)
Salmonberries	nkaal	(*n-koth*)

Other

Mushrooms	k'neat	(*ka-neat*)
Roots (Indian Potatoes)	tsaas	(*choss*)

Made in the USA
Charleston, SC
09 March 2013